BEST
LESBIAN
ROMANCE
2013

BEST
LESBIAN
ROMANCE
2013

Edited by
RADCLYFFE

CLEiS
PRESS

Published in the United States by Cleis Press, Inc., 2246 Sixth Street, Berkeley, California 94710.

Printed in the United States.
Cover design: Scott Idleman/Blink
Cover photograph: Peter Correz/Photodisc
Text design: Frank Wiedemann

First Edition.
10 9 8 7 6 5 4 3 2 1

Trade paper ISBN: 978-1-57344-901-4
E-book ISBN: 978-1-57344-918-2

"Night at the Wax Museum" © Delilah Devlin, *Girls Who Bite*, Cleis Press, 2012. "Lucky Charm," © Kate Dominic, *Lipstick Lovers*, Xcite Books, 2012. "Sgt. Rae" © Sacchi Green, *Duty and Desire*, Cleis Press, 2012.

CONTENTS

INTRODUCTION

"Love" and "romance" are often used interchangeably to describe the state of deep emotional and physical connection between two individuals. While the concept is similar, the nuances are distinct—love is an emotion, whereas romance might be the process that leads to love or the greater framework by which that love is expressed (hence, the idea of a "lifelong romance"). Love exists in many permutations: between friends, family members, and even members of other species ("love me, love my dog, cat, horse, etc."), but romance is reserved for lovers (and not necessarily just for the young or young at heart). Love and romance sometime grow out of our darkest moments, strengthening and comforting us with possibility, as in Anna Meadows's "The Loneliest Road," when two very different women meet by chance and find they share similar pain. Their meeting and the soul-deep understanding that results offer the promise of a new beginning.

The woman only kissed her back, her mouth as chapped and dry as the cracked ground of the Nevada desert.

> *Lila pulled away just enough to speak, their fore-*
> *heads still touching. "Thank you," she said, though*
> *for what she didn't know. For being willing to die*
> *for her and everybody else, even those who'd sent*
> *her away with nothing but those combat boots. For*
> *keeping a hand on the small of Lila's back, a palm's*
> *width of warmth for when winter settled over the*
> *Great Basin.*

Everyone who has ever loved remembers the first time—the freshness, the wonder, the transformation that throws wide the door to the future and floods us with joy. The young narrator in Joey Bass's "The Color of Autumn" reminds us of the bravery and innocence of first love:

> *The other students in the hallway faded to mere*
> *shadows. I no longer cared who they were or what*
> *they were thinking. I was who I was and Angela Hart*
> *wanted me to follow her. A feeling of great happi-*
> *ness and well-being filled me. It was right…. A part*
> *of me knew I would follow those swaying hips and*
> *that waterfall hair anywhere, and I would be doing*
> *it for years.*

Love changes, just as it transforms us, altering its color and fabric and design as life weaves its imprint. Inevitably, love changes the course of our lives in the most unexpected ways. Sometimes, we risk everything for the promise of that lifelong romance. In Andrea Dale's "The Last Rays of the Summer Sun," the essence of long-term love is celebrated.

I fell besotted and breathless once again with the curve of her collarbone, the dusky hardness of her nipples, the rounded pooch of her belly, the softness of her inner arm as I stroked it with my fingertips.

I felt dizzy with desire in a way I'd forgotten, and hadn't realized I'd forgotten until now.

Love and romance may defy simple definition, but every story in this collection speaks to the universal thread that binds lovers everywhere—possibility. As you travel through these love stories, I hope you remember the first wondrous steps of the journey and dream of the next to come.

Radclyffe
2013

HOME TO HER COUNTRY

Cheyenne Blue

Her face was as hard, brown and unyielding as the dirt on which she stood.

I came to a stop in front of Ana and waited for her to crack a smile, for her face to fold into welcoming lines. "Say something," I begged.

She leaned the hayfork against the tree. "You must have been to the house. How did you understand my mother? She doesn't speak a word of English."

I swallowed. I hadn't expected her to fall into my arms cooing with delight, but I'd hoped for more than this.

"I learned some Spanish. I had time after you left."

Time enough to cry, to clean the house, to arrange the clothes and books Ana had left behind in among my own, so that if she came back she'd feel like she belonged with me. Time to take both a basic and an intermediate Spanish course.

She answered me with a stream of Spanish that was cruel and telling in its speed. I picked up single words and simple phrases in the torrent: "Back to America" and "I live here." But I'd come so far to see her, thought about this for so long, that I wasn't going to be easily put off.

"You left without telling me why," I said. "If I can't have you back, I'd like an explanation."

Her façade cracked for the briefest instant, and I saw a flash of softness in her brown eyes.

"Sometimes it's easier not to say anything."

"Easier for you maybe. Not for me. You hurt me, Ana. I came home and you were just gone. No note, no message. Just a hole in my life where you used to be. I spent the first week convinced you'd be back. The second trying to find where you were. You didn't tell anyone."

"How did you find me?"

"The airline rang asking if you'd complete a survey about your flight to Madrid. You gave our—my—number for contact. I realized you must have gone to visit your home village."

"I'm not visiting—I live here now." Her face cracked a mirthless smile. "But of course you must know that as you speak Spanish so well."

The heat of the midday sun beat down on my head, and my face was burning from more than the scorn of her words. "Your mother gave me your lunch. Seems you left without it this morning."

"Every morning. Mother...forgets things sometimes."

I'd seen the vagueness in her mother's milky eyes when she'd wordlessly pressed a package into my hands.

There was a blanket spread in the sparse shade of an olive tree. Without waiting for Ana's invitation, I sat and rested my back against the tree's sharp bark. The lunch pack contained a crusty loaf, some sort of hard white cheese, olives, tomatoes and a rich dark fig, which had cracked, spreading sticky sweetness over the bread. It was a lunch for one, not two, but I broke the bread in half anyway, pairing it with thick slices of the cheese.

Ana sat too, her back to the tree. Our shoulders touched, but it wasn't companionable. I stole a glance at her as she bit into the food. She'd lost weight since she left the States; any soft edges had been honed into muscle. Not the calculated stature of a gym rat, but the blunt lines of a manual worker. Her dark hair was pulled from her face by a yellow bandana, and she wore a pair of cropped cotton pants and a khaki tank top. Her skin gleamed through a fine layer of dust. She'd been working when I found her, following the vague gesture from her mother, an hour from the village, turning hay. A couple of pale stalks clung to her tank top.

I divided the fig into two. Juice coated my fingers, and as I handed Ana her half, our fingers touched: hers dry, rough and hot, mine sticky and pale. We didn't talk. When she'd finished her meager lunch—made smaller by my presence—she rose to her feet and stomped back to the hay. I remained in the shade of the tree, watching as she turned her back to me and started down the row of hay, methodically forking as she went. Sweat gleamed on her shoulders and the dust from her efforts rose in the air and settled on her skin.

This was her life now, it seemed. A small village, where cars were too wide for the tight stone streets. Where doors were open in the afternoon sun and women came out to beat rugs and sweep steps. Where every open door showed the same tiled floor and heavy wooden furniture. This wasn't Madrid, or Barcelona, or Seville, or any Spanish town where the tourists swarmed. This was a simple way of life, one that was passing swiftly from Europe.

I knew Ana mourned its passing. Often, when we'd lain in bed together in our Seattle apartment, she'd told me of her life growing up: cooking with her mother, long lazy days in the hills with the sheep and goats, a ten-year-old child with only the fierce dogs for company—dogs that would protect her as well as the sheep. Days spent picking olives, tending the vegetable garden and cooking, always cooking. But it was one thing to look back on a childhood with fondness and wistfulness; it was another to give up her current life to retreat to nostalgia.

Ana propped her pitchfork against the tree, picked up the water skin, and took a long draft. Wordlessly, I rose and took up her fork and continued down the row of drying grass, mimicking her actions. I wasn't as proficient as she was, and the stalks fell in haphazard lines.

She watched me for a moment before coming over. "Here," she said in a gruff voice. "Hold the fork lower, near the prongs. You'll have more control over the movement." Her warm hand covered mine as she slid it down the handle.

She was right, and my row became neater, although it was still a disaster compared to hers. I forked grimly for twenty minutes or so. My back ached from the unaccustomed bending and I oozed sweat in the heat. But I'd come thousands of miles to talk to her, and if some manual labor would smooth the path, then so be it.

I reached the end of the row and looked back. For a moment I couldn't see her, then I spied the yellow bandana. She was stretched on the blanket on her stomach, her head resting on folded arms. I walked over. The sunlight dappled her skin through the scanty shade of gray-green leaves. She was asleep. I squatted down, able to study her in a way I daren't when she was awake. Her dark hair curled out of the back of the bandana, wisps of it stuck to her neck. Her skin was darker than it had been in the States. Now she was burnished to a rich copper. Ana exhaled deeply and shifted onto her side, but didn't waken. I studied her high-boned face, the way her thick eyelashes made dark crescents on her face. My hand moved, hovered. I wanted to touch her, to remember how she'd felt underneath my hands in our other life, but I was afraid of waking her.

For a moment, I thought about lying down with her, curling my body to hers, but her earlier prickliness dissuaded me. Instead, I went back out into sunshine so bright it washed the color from the landscape, and picked up the fork again.

It was probably an hour later when Ana came up behind me, startling me as she touched my shoulder.

"You've done enough," she said. "You'll be very stiff tomorrow."

In truth, I was one big burning ache now. I had a blister on one hand, and my face flamed with the heat.

She touched one finger to my nose. "You're burning. You should have rested the siesta, as I did."

I didn't answer, just followed her back to where our packs rested together in a closeness their owners didn't share. Ana picked hers up, swinging it onto her shoulders.

"I'm going to bring in the flock," she said. "You better come too."

I swung my own pack onto my shoulders, wincing as it banged my aching back, gritted my teeth and marched doggedly in Ana's wake.

We found the flock spread over a mountain pasture, a mix of sinewy, scraggy sheep and goats. A rangy dog was with them. He had a shaggy coat and gimlet eyes, and barely spared me a glance before focusing all his attention on Ana. She issued a series of sharp commands, and the dog took off at a flat-out run. Ana rested on her staff, looking every inch the rustic shepherd, and waited, occasionally issuing a piercing sequence of whistles. In no time, the animals plunged past with nervous eyes, the dog at their heels.

We set off down the mountain, striding down the path we'd plodded up earlier. Ana took her flock into the village, where she and the dog penned them into the area underneath the house. It was pungent with the musty smell of hay and their droppings.

Only then did she turn to me again. "You better come home with me."

I hadn't given much thought to where to stay, but it was obvious the village had no *pensione*, certainly no comfortable hotel.

Ana strode off again, not into the house, but around the twisting stone streets of the village. She bought bread in one shop, meat at an unmarked doorway, milk at another. Only then did she lead me home.

Her mother greeted us with a vague smile, never asking what I was doing with her daughter, and Ana offered no explanation. She hugged her mother and launched into a stream of Spanish, too fast for me to follow, although I caught words about dinner and the weather.

Ana took her mother by the arm and led her into another room. After a moment of indecision, I followed.

Once past the doorway, the smell of urine was strong. Ana's mother's face twisted in anguish, and she started to cry in a silent, helpless sort of way.

"*Lo siento,*" she said, over and over. *I'm sorry.*

Ana pinched the bridge of her nose briefly, and smiled at her mother. "*De nada.*" *It's nothing.* She ushered her mother to a recliner, the only piece of modern furniture in the room, helping her to sit, adjusting the footrest with a precision that told me she'd done it many times before. She flicked on the TV and handed her mother the remote. Only when her mother was smiling at a game show did she leave.

Back in the kitchen she brushed past me as I stood awkwardly in the middle of the room. Antiseptic splashed into a bucket, water and a cloth.

"Let me," I said.

Her eyes flashed. *"Es mi madre."* That I understood: she is *my* mother.

As I watched her, the long flight and the emotion of the day caught up with me. My head spun with tiredness and all I wanted to do was sleep. One hand on the doorjamb, I closed my eyes for a moment. When I opened them, Ana was watching me.

"Come," she said.

The room she took me to was obviously hers. The single bed was rumpled, and clothes were scattered on the floor. The only other furniture was a heavy wooden chair and a chest of drawers.

"Sleep. We'll talk in the morning."

"It's your bed," I started to say, but she pushed me on the shoulder so that I sat heavily on the side. *"No hay otra cama." There is no other bed.*

Too tired to undress properly, I fell asleep to the sound of clattering pots from the kitchen.

My body clock was still on American time, so I woke to the sound of soft snoring. The room was dark. Ana was spooned behind me in the narrow bed, her face pressed into the curve of my neck and shoulder. Her arm was heavy across my waist and I could see her hand lying palm up and fingers loosely curled.

Memories engulfed me, so abruptly, so intensely, that for a moment I couldn't find my breath. Although we were both semi-clothed, Ana's breasts pushed into my back and her knees nudged the backs of my thighs. I took a deep, slow breath, and even though I needed to pee and my stomach rumbled with hunger, I didn't want to disturb this moment. The months alone in America eased away, and in the dark night, I could pretend that Ana and I were still together, that any moment I could turn to her, kiss her awake and explore her body with fingers and tongue. I'd missed this—missed her—so very much.

Although I was trying hard not to move, she probably sensed the change from sleep to awake. She snuffled in her sleep, and her hand curled around my breast, cupping it. She'd often slept that way, mimicking the curve of my body with her own. I lay without moving for a long, long time, savoring the touch of her body against mine.

I must have fallen asleep again, because I woke to the absence of her. I sat up and she was sitting on the end of the bed, pulling on her sandals. For a moment, we stared at each other. It was probably my imagination, but I thought that some of the softness of the night lingered in her eyes. With a nod she was gone, down the hall, and I heard her speaking to her mother. There was so much love in her voice it made my throat ache.

I found the bathroom on my third try and had a quick wash standing up at the basin. There was no shower, just a heavy iron bath in the corner, but the bright blue tiles and terra-cotta floor were sparkling clean.

I found Ana and her mother in the kitchen. They were sitting at the table eating breakfast—or rather Ana was. Her mother was moving a sweet pastry around her plate, destroying it with her fingers until there was nothing but crumbs.

There was a third plate with a pastry and a small cup of strong black coffee. No milk. In the States, I would have demanded another coffee, a larger one with cream, but here I drank it. Ana watched me, and I thought I caught a flicker of approval on her face at my lack of complaint.

"¿Quién es?" asked her mother, and her eyes snapped to my face with an abruptness and clarity I'd assumed she'd lost.

"*Mi amiga*, Vika," replied Ana.

Her mother's eyes ran over my face and plain gray T-shirt. "*Se viste como un niño.*" *She dresses like a boy.* She wadded the crumbs on her plate into a ball and stuffed them into her mouth, chewing ferociously.

"*I* dress like a boy," said Ana, in Spanish.

"But you are...you are like a boy." As suddenly as the clarity was there, it was gone, her brown eyes clouding like the milky coffee I longed for.

We ate in silence, but my thoughts ran in heated, chaotic circles. Why Ana had returned was obvious, and I dared to assume that she'd run out on me rather than explain. But what would happen now?

The pastry was flaky and sweet, and melted on my tongue. I finished and rose, collecting my plate and those of Ana and her mother. I washed them in the sink, leaving them to drain on the side, and then, without a word, found food for lunch: bread, some of the hard white cheese and thin slices of smoked ham. I packed them into two containers and added a couple of oranges from a bowl on the dresser.

I returned to the dining room and put our lunches into the daypack I'd seen Ana use the day before. Ana watched silently, then turned on the TV and assisted her mother to the chair. After kissing her mother on her crêpey cheek, she left, with me trailing in her wake like a comet's tail.

The pack banged my shoulders, which were stiff from yesterday's exertion, but I forced myself to keep up with Ana as she whistled for the dog and let the small flock out from underneath the house.

The day was a repeat of yesterday. We walked steadily to the upper pastures where Ana whistled a series of commands to the dog, which dropped to the ground, eyes never leaving the animals. Ana and I spent the morning turning the hay so that the damp underside was exposed to the sun. This time I took siesta with Ana, stretching out with her on the blanket. She was asleep in moments, but it took me longer, unaccustomed as I was to napping in the middle of the day. I lay on my side, watching her brown shoulders rise and fall slightly with her breathing. I could hear the buzz of a fly and far away the bleating of the goats, which faded as I slipped into sleep.

In the afternoon, we forked the hay into conical stacks. Ana was neat and efficient, but my attempts often left the hay floating haphazardly to the ground. Despite her promise of the night before, there was little conversation between us. I'd decided I'd wait for her to make the first move, so apart from necessary instructions and requests, we were silent.

We arrived back to the house to find her mother still in front of the blaring TV. After dinner, which Ana cooked, I cleaned up while Ana sat with her mother, holding her hands, talking to her in soft tones. I watched them while trying to appear engrossed in the dishes. Ana's love was deep-rooted, that was obvious, and once, when I glanced up, I saw her mother smiling softly back at her.

My hands stilled in the sink. What was I doing here? I should go home, back to America. It was obvious Ana would never leave her mother, and I wasn't sure there was a place for me in her life, even if she wanted me to stay. I held a tourist visa that expired in five weeks. I had a flight back to Seattle and my college courses waiting for me.

I stared openly at the scene in the living room. Ana looked away from her mother for a moment and our eyes locked. I don't know what she saw in my expression, in that moment of despair, but she smiled, a warm, genuine Ana smile, different from the tight-lipped snarls she'd offered me before. In that moment, seeing her so beautiful, so strong, so caring, my heart plunged off the precipice again, diving deeper into love, deeper into this woman. At that moment, I made a decision: I would stay until my return flight. I would savor and enjoy this time with Ana while I could, storing memories for the times that would follow without her. And then I would return to the States, without complaint, without tears, without making it difficult for her. I owed her that much.

Later, when her mother had been assisted to bed, Ana asked if I would like to go down to the village for a glass of wine. It was after ten, but I already knew how late the Spanish kept their evenings. Indeed, our early dinner was only in deference to Ana's mother, who liked to retire early to bed.

We left the house, walking through the narrow streets, twisting and turning through the houses until we came to the single café, ablaze with light. It was crowded, people sitting at tables with carafes of wine and small plates of *tapas* in front of them. I sat at a table out on the footpath and Ana disappeared, reappearing in a short time with a carafe of wine and a plate of tiny tastes of food—octopus, some thick yellow tortilla, and some sort of meat in a red sauce.

The wine was heavy and dark, a rich red, and the initial roughness gave way to a throat-warming smoothness. Ana fiddled with her napkin and picked at the tortilla. I waited, figuring that finally, now was the time to talk. With my decision made as to my course of action, all I was hoping for was some acknowledgment of what I had meant to her. Closure, and then maybe, for the rest of my time in Spain, we could recapture some of the closeness we'd shared previously.

"I'm sorry," Ana said eventually. "I should never have run out on you. But I didn't think you'd understand. I thought you would argue, try to change my mind. This is something I have to do." She took my hand across the table. "I loved you, Vika, I did. I could have stayed with you and been happy. Finished my college course. Made a life over there."

I stared at our hands, as intertwined as our lives were now separate. "I loved you too," I said. "I still do. That's why I'm here, but it's not enough, is it?"

Her silence was answer enough. She raised my hand to her lips and kissed the back of it, one of her endearing old-fashioned gestures I remembered so well. Tears prickled at the back of my eyes.

"I can't ask you to wait for me," she said eventually. "It could be...years."

I nodded in understanding.

"What will you do now?" she asked, and her fingers caressed the back of my hand.

"I have five weeks before term starts," I said. "I'd like to stay—if that's okay?"

"I'd like that," she said in low tones. "I've missed you." And then we were hugging, clasping each other tightly, my face in her shoulder, hers in my hair, and we were crying and kissing and crying some more because it was all so right, and so perfect, and we were in love, and it was all so sad and doomed and in five weeks it would be over.

That night we made love in her single bed, coming together silently in the moonlight that streamed through the window. We made love with lips and tongues and voice, and our sweat and tears and juices mingled in a salty sea of passion.

The days took on a rhythm. We would awaken, spooned together in the narrow bed, and Ana would assist her mother while I showered, and then I'd put together breakfast and keep a steady flow of conversation and an eye on her mother while Ana showered. Gradually, her mother came to recognize me, at least some of the time, even once calling me by name. Then, when her mother was settled for the day with her TV and magazines, and a neighbor arranged to check on her and feed her lunch, Ana and I would get on with the simple manual tasks of farming: tending the animals, forking hay, harvesting the olive crop. There were market days in the village, and then we bought food that was not normally available in the small village shop. Once every week, a local teenager would tend to the animals and Ana and I would load the rattling truck with produce and go and sell olives and vegetables direct to the factory in the nearest town. Ana taught me to milk the goats, and then how to turn that milk into a rustic cheese, which we sometimes ate with our dinner.

I discovered the village had a good Internet connection, thanks to a Spanish government initiative, and I was able to keep in touch with friends and family in the States. I made a tentative inquiry about distance learning with my college, but although they told me it was possible, there was still the matter of a Spanish visa.

In the evenings, the two of us would sit with her mother, and I would cook while Ana assisted with her personal care. Sometimes after dinner, we'd go out for a glass of wine, where we were treated with a sort of kind, baffled warmth, that said although we were an oddity being a lesbian couple, it was not something to disapprove of.

And at night, in the narrow bed, we made sweet love, fierily passionate love and energetic lustful love.

"Are you happy here?" Ana asked one day.

I was squatting on the wooden milking stool, my head pressed into the goat's flank. My nose was full of the goat's pungent odor, and straw tickled my feet. Ana's words distracted me from the fiddly task of milking.

My immediate reaction was to say *of course*. But when I glanced up and saw her serious expression, I paused and gave more consideration to my answer.

"I love being with you," I said, "but I think I could be happy in most places if you were with me. But here?" I sorted through my thoughts. "Yes. I'm happy. It's not what I expected—it's quieter, less frantic, but I like the rhythm of life."

Two weeks until I had to leave. Ana and I had fallen into a happy routine. My Spanish had improved—enough that Ana would send me alone to the shop and know that I would return with more or less the correct items. We'd spent a couple of evenings with a friend of Ana's and her husband, and for the most part, I was able to follow the conversation. They were kind enough to speak slowly, and tentatively, I would join in.

One week left, and my departure loomed. I started cataloging the little things to remember when I was back in the States: the loud shout of laughter Ana gave when I mangled the language, the quiet moments together on the balcony overlooking the village with a glass of the rich, rough red wine. The bustle of market day, the sense of achievement when I found a goat that had strayed, the feeling of protectiveness and care when Ana's mother called me by my name and held my hand to her cheek. And of course our lovemaking: sweet, hot, intense. How Ana would forget to breathe as her orgasm approached. The taste of her on my tongue and fingers. Her dark head at my breast. Our limbs entwined, sated and relaxed after lovemaking.

Three days before my departure, Ana came in holding a thick, official-looking envelope. I was sitting with her mother, encouraging her to eat, but Ana's posture alerted me. She put the envelope carefully down on the table and sat down next to me.

"Vika," she began, "you know I love you, right?"

I nodded and disentangled my hands from her mother's, and

Ana immediately claimed one. "Would you stay here with me, Vika? With us, me and mom?"

My world narrowed to her intense, serious expression. How long did she mean? An extra week? A month? A year? *Forever?*

She must have seen my hesitation, as she opened the envelope. The familiar crest of my American college was on the letterhead. "You can finish your degree via distance learning. Or you can transfer to the university in Burgos, one hour away. You can even get a minor in Spanish."

My gaze was riveted on the tremble in her fingers.

"I've thought of that. Even made similar enquiries. But I don't have a visa for that long, and I don't think a student visa would—"

"Marry me, Vika." Her words cut through my fumbling explanation. Tiny words. Short and sharp, but they shafted deep to pierce my unarticulated dreams and desires. *If only*, I thought. *If only.*

Ana must have seen my anguished expression, because she smiled slightly. "We may still have goats under the house, but Spain allows us to marry, as openly, officially and joyously as any straight couple."

I'd forgotten that, if indeed I'd ever known.

It was as if the sun had lodged itself in my chest and was now expanding with the morning. Would I marry my love? I opened my mouth to say, yes, yes, yes, a million times yes, when Ana's mother shuffled in her seat. Slowly she pushed herself to her feet. Her eyes were as clear and sharp as I'd ever seen them.

"Vika," she said. "Vika, marry my daughter. Please."

It was settled.

WHERE THE GIRLS ARE

Ariel Graham

Sandra went to the city because there was nowhere else to go. It wasn't supposed to be a huge change. The city was only Reno, Nevada, a population even with outlying communities that was still well under half a million. Still, it was a City with capital letters compared to the desert community of Fernley, forty miles to the east and simmering in the desert sun.

She went to the city because her marriage was over and she thought there had to be more out there than a farming community and two grocery stores, a place where Starbucks didn't arrive until the new century was more than half a dozen years under way, and where if you knew anybody—and she knew everybody at this point, even the California imports—they knew you.

Or they thought they knew you. She was pretty sure even she didn't know Sandra, not after so long living with Dave and the day-to-day idiocy of his life. She'd tried. She had loved him, once, many long football games and beer-soaked poker games ago, before the small yappy dogs he began collecting. Before he started ignoring her.

Before she'd learned something about Sandra by accident. The morning she'd joined the new gym in Fernley and discovered a locker room full of women who didn't bother with towels or modesty—and most of them should have, she thought. She'd always watched her weight, always worked out and eaten conservatively, and she wasn't one of the ones prancing around without a towel.

But she liked watching, especially the women with hard bodies, lean and long from physical work on farms, tanned by the sun, and equally the few who were gym-toned and tanning-bed tanned. And she told Dave, much later, with great hesitancy, and suggested maybe since two women was every man's fantasy, so-called... Only turned out Dave didn't have a lot of fantasies. It wasn't Sandra who left him cold, it was pretty much the whole messy business of sex.

She took to reading personal ads. She dreamed of women. She daydreamed of women. She worked out harder and longer, and spent more time in the locker room than she needed to, but nobody looked at her twice, except people who knew her, and those she wasn't about to engage. If she did anything in Fernley, all of Fernley would know. So when Dave finally called it quits—politely, kindly, but still without passion—and offered her the house, the dogs (his dogs), the whole nine yards, she said thank you, but she was going to move to the city.

"Sacramento?" Dave asked. "Or San Francisco?"

She looked at him sharply, trying to judge if he was teasing her, or angry, or sarcastic, or even if he'd figured out what she hadn't told him and certainly hadn't told herself.

"I thought I'd start with Reno before I moved to Paris," she said lightly and he blinked before smiling.

"I didn't mean to hurt you," Dave said.

"You didn't," Sandra said. "But you ignored me, and that did hurt."

That night they slept together for the last time. Since he was keeping the house and the dogs and the life she didn't want, she'd start looking for somewhere to live in the morning. It was a long night, listening to Dave snore and mutter and fighting both excitement and fear until she realized neither could be banished and neither was going to allow her to sleep and so she gave into both. She imagined meeting tall, strong, raw-muscled women, the kind of take-charge, experienced women who would know what she needed and look after her, the kind of short-haired, strong women Dave looked at with disdain, too manly, too butch.

Before she finally slept, which was just before dawn, she wondered, briefly, very briefly, if she was trading one Dave for another. But she didn't know the lifestyle and she had nothing else to compare anything to but the life she'd led.

Which was why she was excited. And afraid.

In the morning, she moved to Reno.

"You're new here, aren't you?" the bartender asked. She looked maybe a day over twenty-one, wore a wedding ring and a ponytail.

"I'm new everywhere," Sandy said. She'd ordered a white wine, because she never drank it, then remembered that was because it gave her a headache.

The bartender nodded. "You still have a tan line from the wedding ring." Whoever it was she assumed Sandy had left, she didn't ask. "Want to know who to look out for?"

"Oh, no, please, I'd much rather find out the hard way,"

Sandy said, and ruined it by laughing at the bartender's startled expression.

"Some people would." She dried a row of glasses and set them on racks under a mirrored stand of more alcohols than Sandy could name. The bar was dusky but not dark. Dust motes filled errant sunbeams. There were the requisite pool tables and dartboards, scattered tables and booths and of course stools at the bar. The juke was so quiet she couldn't hear what was playing, although earlier she could have sworn she'd heard Metallica.

The bartender nodded at a couple of women in the corner booth sitting together. "The harpies. Don't ask me their names, because I can't ever remember. They like to take people home with them and then they end up bitterly angry if the third person doesn't exactly follow the script they've got in their heads. And that's Bebe," she said, nodding at a round woman who had been headed their way but abruptly veered off. "She owes everybody in this place, and not just drinks."

"What else could she owe them?" Sandy wondered aloud.

The bartender gave her a look that said Sandy was pulling her leg. "Money. What else?" She took a look all the way around the bar and said, "That's mostly it. It's a good crowd, those I know."

Sandy took her own look, spinning on her stool. She'd spun almost all the way around when she saw the girl. "And who's she?"

The bartender followed her glance and frowned. The honey blonde sat with her back to them, a quarter of the way around the bar from Sandy, slim and young and wearing jeans.

The bartender shrugged. "Guess I don't know everyone," she said and the girl turned around and Sandy fell in love.

The juke kicked up while Sandy made the thousand-mile trek from her own stool to the blonde's. Suddenly some kind of rock song blew up, all drums and bass and very loud, and Sandy's heart beat louder and faster than the music. Just before she reached the girl, she thought about turning around and running. Just turn around and go back to her own stool. She was older and she'd never done this and she wasn't sure what to—

The girl spun back around. Cute, and kind of kittenish. Old enough to drink, young enough to look aware of doing so.

At second glance she wasn't that young, maybe thirty to Sandy's thirty-seven. The honey blond looked natural and her lips were pink and soft, her eyes big and blue. She wasn't at all Sandy's repeated fantasies during the apartment hunt, the move, the job search and the slow explorations of where to go to meet people. Instead she was younger, softer and maybe even more uncertain than Sandy—who realized she was standing and staring as if looking at another personal ad rather than a person.

"Can I buy you a drink?" She winced. Smooth. The blonde already had a drink, something straight and amber.

The blonde shook her head. "How about some company? I'm Emily."

Of course you are. The name fit her, all drawing rooms and pink roses. What was she doing here? "Sandy."

"Tina," Emily called, "get Sandy another of whatever she's drinking?" Because Sandy had wandered off from her drink, left the white wine sitting unattended on the bar.

"Actually, let me switch to red," Sandy said. "I always forget white wine gives me a headache."

Emily said, "I have two Labradors and an MFA I have no use for. I work for my brother's law office because otherwise his practice would fall apart and I'd have to support him, because he has no common sense and never pays his bills on time, not because he can't afford to but because he can't remember to. My parents live back east, only I grew up out here. I'm allergic to cats, mint and Crest toothpaste, though that last may be a preference. I've read everything Stephen King has ever written and one of my main goals in life is never to climb Mount Everest, which, so far, I'm doing rather well at. Now your turn."

Sandy gaped at her. "What?"

Emily grinned, and in that moment was less Vassar and pink roses and more an urchin on the street, ill-behaved but entertaining. "What's your life story?"

"You want the boring version or the good stuff?"

Emily shrugged. "Which is which?" She nodded thanks at the bartender, sliding Sandy's red wine to her.

"The boring version is the truth. Isn't that always the way?" The music was turning up in the bar but she was afraid to shout over it, certain it would end abruptly when she said something embarrassing.

"No," Emily said, "but I'm sorry if it seems that way. Tell me both versions."

Sandy raised her brows, thought briefly. "I'm deposed royalty from a small European nation no one has ever heard of and came here to learn the ways of the American West in hopes of fitting in, finding a new life and avoiding the royal assassins who were sent to make sure I never made another bid for the throne. I have no intention of making a bid for the throne because thrones are wildly uncomfortable."

Emily, who had asked for the interesting version, stared at Sandy as if she were mad, then said, "I should have said I was a vampire. It would explain why I'm so pale, and anyway, now I sound so boring. Do you want to get out of here?"

"Yes."

They walked along the Truckee River, Reno's claim to fame on the subject of cities with rivers running through them, into the arts and culture district of Reno and out the other side through a tree-crowded park and up past the city's arts and culture building and even farther along the river. There were people along the river, people in kayaks as the sun began to lower and shadows deepened, and people fishing and people throwing sticks for dogs. Other couples strolled and no one seemed to notice Sandy holding hands with Emily.

When the river ducked under an overpass, Emily pulled Sandy under the road and pushed her against the concrete. Her mouth on Sandy's was hard and spicy, tasting of whatever she'd last been drinking. Her lips were softer than Dave's, smooth, and it felt strange not to have stubble brushing her cheek. It felt strange, actually, to be touched, after having gone so long without. Everything in Sandy's body responded. Her breath came faster. Her nipples hardened. Heat seemed to radiate from her body. Between her legs she ached, wet and open and ready.

Emily kissed her mouth, hard, bit Sandy's lip, slid her tongue deep into Sandy's mouth. Her hands slid down from Sandy's shoulders to her breasts, her palms pressing flat in slow, deep circles around the nipples. She eased one leg between Sandy's and at the same time pressed herself against Sandy's thigh.

I don't know what to do, Sandy thought, panicked.

But Emily did. Whatever experience she'd had, she knew to kiss and nibble at Sandy's lips, work her way down Sandy's jawline, to her earlobes, her neck, along her collarbones, and down the front of the button-up Sandy wore.

And Sandy let go. Years ago, when she'd first married, and before that, when she'd first dated, it had all been so easy, natural. She touched and was touched and everything around her was experience. Everything was new and soft and out of time. There was nothing to worry about. It was mutual touching, hands and lips and tongues.

She leaned into Emily's kiss, her own tongue snaking out to touch Emily's, to lick along Emily's lips. Her hands came up and molded themselves around firm breasts, felt nipples pressing hard from the jersey of Emily's T-shirt and she pressed, rubbed her palms flat over Emily's breasts, feeling them rise to meet her touch, hard, little erections. She brought her fingers together and pinched, gently, pulling them against the thin fabric of the shirt, and all the while her lips continued to explore and Emily ground against her thigh. Slowly Emily's hands began wandering down Sandy's body, probably feeling hardened nipples inside bra and oxford shirt. Emily cupped her hands under Sandy's breasts, her thumbs meeting at Sandy's sternum, as if she weighed the flesh against her hands or simply marveled at it and framed it. She took her mouth away from Sandy's and leaned to blow against the shirt, against the nipples, opening her mouth wide so her breath was hot against fabric and flesh. Her hands slipped down Sandy's rib cage, along her waist, dropped lower and began pressing against Sandy's pussy, cupping her crotch through the blue jeans, thumbing clit and pressing fingers hard and straight against pussy, pressing upward. She rubbed, twice.

Sandy came, explosively hard, the way she had in the early days of sex, in those moments she'd imagined the high school stud she was with was one of the cheerleaders. She'd forgotten that fantasy. It made her smile against Emily's neck as they stood pressed together under the bridge. They stood still, within the shadows, listening to the flow of traffic overhead on Reno's streets, to people only yards away, walking dogs, jogging in the late-summer evening.

"Come home with me," Emily whispered. "Let me—"

"You come with me," Sandy said. "Come to my place. It's new. I'm new. I want to make you feel like you just made me feel."

Emily smiled. Pink cheeks, bright blue eyes. "All right."

Sandy's place wasn't hers yet. She'd signed all the leases, the background check, the credit checks. She had the keys and she'd been there about a week. But it was still white-walled, free of ornamentation. It said nothing about who lived there. Nothing had imprinted.

Emily wandered to the double French doors and stared out at the pint-sized backyard. "What will you plant?"

She hadn't thought about it yet. Now she said, "Honeysuckle. Morning glories. Wisteria."

Emily laughed. "This is Nevada. You like a challenge?"

Sandy nodded. "Oh, yes."

Her new bed was her. Not yet broken in but beautiful. A four-poster, with dark wood and delicate chiffons trailing from a crisscross that nearly formed a canopy. Ornate scrollwork along the brass rails above the bed from which the chiffon draped. A big bed, meant to be lacy and girly, but she'd been cold sleeping alone and there was a Tinker Bell fleece blanket in the middle of the unmade bed.

Emily said, "I think this is you."

"You don't know me." Sandy stood behind her, nearly touching but not quite. She could feel the heat coming off her.

"I'm hopeful. Indulge me." Emily turned with a laugh on her face but her eyes went serious when they met Sandy's.

"All right."

Sandy undressed Emily as she might unwrap a gift. As if she wished for more layers between them so that the unveiling spun out, long and hot and sensual. In fact, Emily wore a T-shirt over firm, large breasts. No bra. No undershirt. Just pale, creamy flesh, like the delicate paleness of her cheeks. Her nipples were hard, rose colored, upturned. Sandy touched them as if expecting them to dart away, like butterflies, tested them with her tongue, lapped around them, suddenly took them in her mouth as if she couldn't stand not to any longer and Emily laughed, unexpected, wound her hands in Sandy's hair and let her head fall back, her eyes mostly closed.

Sandy kissed her way down Emily's flat belly, let her tongue follow the line of Emily's jeans. Emily herself shoved them down and off, only jeans, tight, faded, and under them, Emily, no underwear, no G-string. Sandy kicked the jeans away and Emily moved to the bed, her hands linked with Sandy's, her eyes linked with Sandy's. She sank down, onto the bed, her legs parted, her gaze on Sandy's. "Make love to me."

I don't know how. Panic again, bright wings of it in her mind.

"I can hear what you're thinking," Emily said.

Sandy, so far gone, froze. Not believing. Still, somehow, believing Emily could.

"Not like that," Emily said. "I mean…You said you're new. You haven't done this. I'm new to you. Women." She leaned up from the bed and grinned at Sandy, looking like a kid, like every high school fantasy Sandy had ever had about cheerleaders. "Just do everything you ever wanted anyone to do to you," she said. "Experiment. Take your time. I don't mind. I'm the perfect test subject. I'll just lie back and—well, let you work things out."

And Sandy laughed. The tight panic in her chest blew away. *Do everything you ever wanted anyone to do to you.*

She knelt over Emily on the bed, kissing her way down Emily's slim body. She kissed jaw and mouth and earlobes and ran her tongue along the curl of Emily's ear until Emily laughed and twisted away and said it tickled. She nuzzled the hollow in the creamy throat and kissed the length of the collarbone and kissed up the slopes of the hard, firm breasts, sucked nipples into her mouth and heard Emily gasp with pleasure and laughed to herself to think Emily thought she was the one receiving pleasure. She swirled her tongue around the nipples, along the sensitive flesh around them. She kissed and nipped and tasted and played, her fingers stroking through Emily's hair, along her arms, down her rib cage until her hands seemed to lead on their own, down Emily's ribs, along her waist, down the sharp valleys formed by her hipbones. Her hands led her mouth and her mouth followed, tasting salt and sweat and dusky pleasures, down to Emily's carefully trimmed pussy.

She stopped then, for an instant, not afraid, just somehow awed, and Emily twisted under her, nowhere near as patient as she'd said she was. Her hips twisted and bucked and Sandy laughed and held her down with both hands on her sharp, thin hipbones. *Patience*, she thought. *I've waited thirty years for this.*

The shadows crept into the room. The sun had gone down, streetlights were coming on. The long, soft summer evening curled into night. Sandy's tongue stroked down the inside of one hip, along the top of the mons and then slowly, along one side, to the juncture of leg and pussy, and Emily twisted under her, making sounds, and Sandy laughed again, thought, *I know exactly what you're thinking. You're thinking I'm lost. I'm not lost. I'm just—exploring.*

She ran her tongue over the top of Emily's pussy, streaking across the bisected fold where her clit hardened and waited, down the other side of her thigh, lapping lazily, playing at the edge of reason, and then purposefully, with intent, she licked up once, long and hard, from Emily's hot, wet cunt to the very top of her mons and dipped down, found her clit, ran her tongue around the hard bud and sucked it in.

The one thing she'd always been afraid of. That she wouldn't recognize a clit, wouldn't be able to find it, wouldn't know what to do with it. And Emily's clit was under her tongue, between her lips. In her mouth.

She sucked hard and Emily panted and gasped, her hands coming down on either side of Sandy, trying to get at her own pussy. Sandy pushed them away. *I'll take care of that.* But she didn't stop sucking long enough to say anything. Just brought her hands down and used her fingers to open Emily's pussy, pushing flesh back and away, running her fingers down under her sucking mouth, running one and then two and finally three fingers up inside, feeling Emily's silken walls, wet and hot and slick, clutching at her fingers like a hungry mouth.

Just do everything you ever wanted anyone to do to you.

And so she sucked her, and fucked her, and made her writhe, her blond hair splaying out across Sandy's pillow, her hips bucking and thrusting as she pressed herself harder against the fingers inside her, harder and faster, her hips riding the swells and valleys of pleasure.

She came so hard Sandy couldn't have missed it. Came and lay back, still, making small noises. Her fingers fluttered at the edge of her own cunt and now Sandy let her, not knowing what to do to prolong the end of the contractions. Emily only stroked, as if not aware she was touching herself.

The room had grown almost totally dark. Emily was a shadowy stranger Sandy pushed herself up to lie beside, until Emily snuggled into her, a soft, warm weight against Sandy's chest. Sandy stroked her hair and felt something within her melt.

Some daylight still remained outside when Emily stirred, kissed Sandy's shoulder and jaw and throat and mouth and pulled herself up, fishing around the darkened bedroom floor for her clothes.

"You could stay," Sandy said. Her voice sounded flat. She didn't know if she wanted Emily to stay or not.

"I could stay. But I'm not going to." Emily stroked Sandy's cheek in the near darkness and Sandy sat up, realized she was still mostly clothed. "You're new to all this. You said so yourself. You need some time to process. Think." She grinned again, a white flash of teeth in the bedroom. "To miss me."

"And if I do?"

"Miss me? I'm teasing. But I'd like to see you again."

And Sandy thought Emily held her breath then. It made her heart soar. Someone found her attractive. Someone enjoyed spending time with her. Someone wanted to make love with her.

"Me, too," she said simply, and when all the fear tried to flood upward—giving too much of herself too quickly, trusting in a response that might not come, making herself vulnerable—she shot down all the internal voices so fast she didn't think Emily even saw.

"Me, too," she said again, and grinned at Emily.

SGT. RAE

Sacchi Green

Sgt. Rae was so strong she could carry me at a run through gunfire and smoke and exploding mines. Two years later, she's that strong again. With just one hand she can hold me from getting away, no matter how hard I struggle. Even her voice is enough to stop me at a dead run, so it doesn't matter that she can't run anymore. And anyway, I'd never want to run away.

I'm smaller, but I've got my own kind of muscle, even if it doesn't show. A mechanic in an armored tank unit has to be strong just to handle the tools you need, and if you're a woman doing the job you need a whole extra layer of strength. I'm not an army mechanic anymore, but I can still use tools; Sgt. Rae isn't an army sergeant anymore, but she'll always be in charge. At the town hall where she's the police and fire department dispatcher, they tell me she's got the whole place organized like it's never been before.

In our house, or in the town, I'm supposed to just call her Rae these days, and mostly I remember. I'm just Jenny. In the bedroom, we don't need names at all, except to wake each other when the bad dreams come, and whisper that everything's all right now. Or close enough to handle, as long as we're together.

Out here, though, on this trail I've made through the woods and across the stream, we play by my rules, and that means I'm Specialist 2nd Brown and she's the ball-buster staff sergeant, even though neither of us has any use for balls.

She'll be coming along the trail behind me any minute, coming to see what new contraption I've constructed. What she expects is something like the exercise stations I've built for her into every room in the house, chinning bars and railings and handgrips at different levels, and in a way that's right, but with a different twist. She expects I'll want her to order me to drop and do fifty push-ups or sit-ups, or run in place until I'm panting. But this time I want more.

I check the gears and pulleys one more time, even though I already know the tension is set right. It's my own tension that's nearly out of control. The posts and crossbars are rock solid, while I'm shaking in my old fatigues, so nervous and horny that I can't even tell which is which.

I hear the motor now. I could've made it run quieter, but if you've been where I've been, where we've both been, you want to be sure you know what's coming around the bend.

She's crossed the rocky ford in the stream where no regular wheelchair could have gone. I salvaged tracks from old snow-mobiles at the repair shop where I work, and they're as good as any armored tank tracks, even though they're made of Kevlar instead of steel. Fine for this terrain, and even the steel kind got chewed up in the desert sand in Iraq.

Mustn't think about the desert now. Here in New Hampshire, green leaves overhead are beginning to turn orange and red. This stream flows into a river just beyond our house, and we can watch canoes and kayaks pass by. No desert in sight. This is home. We're together. Safe. Except that safe isn't always enough, when you've known—had to know—so much more.

Now I hear Sgt. Rae veering back and forth through the obstacle course, steering the mini-tank around trees, stumps, boulders, right over small logs. With a double set of the tracks on each side, the only way to steer is by slowing one side while accelerating the other, and that takes strength. I think of her big hands on the levers, the bunched muscles of her arms and shoulders, even stronger now than in the army because she insists on a manually powered chair anywhere but in these woods. Gloves help, but her hands get calloused from turning the wheels. Calloused, and rough, even when she tries to be gentle... Anticipation pounds through my cunt.

I kneel on the ground, close my eyes, try to clear my mind—but on the distant bridge over the river a truck backfires, and in spite of the leafy dampness the desert flashes around me again, the clouds of dust, the explosions, the machine-gun fire on that final day. I think of Sgt. Rae's powerful voice, how it cut through the pain and confusion and kept me breathing when I didn't think I could last another second. "Brown!" she bellowed, again and again, coming closer to where the shattered truck cab trapped me. "Brown, damn you, report!" That sound gripped me, forced strength into me, so that I moved, just a little, no matter how much it hurt, and she found me.

I never remember what happened next. I don't think Sgt. Rae does, either, but somebody told me later they found a bent assault rifle barrel nearby, and maybe she levered the truck cab up enough with that to drag me out. I just remember being slung over her shoulder, feeling her run and swerve and run some more, and hearing her voice drilling right through to my heart in a tone I'd never heard before. "Jenny, Jenny...hang on..."

Right then, with bullets still screaming around us, it was like I'd died and woken up to a new world. Ever since the day we met, Sgt. Rae had mesmerized me, obsessed me, and I'd worked to hide my foolish longings behind hard work and casual jokes and chatter. But in that moment, as her strong voice shook, a window opened in the midst of hell and gave me a glimpse of a heaven better than anything they'd ever preached about in church.

I passed out when she set me down behind a sand bunker some of our guys had piled up in a hurry. Maybe I heard somebody say another soldier was still out there, or maybe I just heard later how she went back into that hell. Either way, I know she went.

It was a month before I saw Sgt. Rae again. I was still bandaged but up and walking. She wasn't. At first, when I stood beside the hospital bed, I wondered whether she was really there at all, inside, until she saw me.

"Jenny?"

I could scarcely hear the word. But then strength came back into her voice, and the power I'd always felt surrounding her was there again as though a light had been switched on. "Specialist Brown, report!"

So I did, listing my injuries and treatments and recovery, even though her half smile softened the formal order. Later, when she'd had her meds and fallen asleep, I pumped the nurses about her injuries and prognosis, and from that day I was never away from her for more than a few hours. There were some rough parts, and sometimes I had to be the strong one to get her through. A nurse or two caught on that there was more to it than just that she'd saved my life, but they never made any fuss. It helped that I could fix mechanical glitches in the orthopedic ward's equipment and even make some things work better than originally designed. I think somewhere along the line they claimed me as an adjunct physical therapy technician.

The dampness of the ground soaking through my jeans brings me back to the present. Sgt. Rae is coming around the clump of hemlock saplings. It's time, and now I'm ready, in position, on my knees, hands clasped high above my head, ropes wrapped around my wrists, head bowed.

"Brown!"

I can't salute in this position, but I try to sound as though I were doing it. "Sergeant, yes Sergeant!"

"What do you think you're doing, Brown?"

"Sergeant, I'm kneeling, Sergeant."

"I can see that. But do you *know* what you're doing?"

Without looking I can tell she's surveying the situation. A pair of leather-wrapped rings hangs right where she can stretch up and reach them. The system of gears and pulleys is rigged to offer just the right amount of resistance and stability for her to pull herself to a standing position, brace with forearms at chest level on a crossbar, and then lower her weight slowly back down. Three of the doorways in our house have similar setups, but this one is more complex—and in this one, the counterweight is me.

"Sergeant, yes Sergeant, I do know what I'm doing."

There's the slightest of creaks as she begins to rise. The ropes tighten, and I rise, too, until I'm dangling in the air, helpless—or as helpless as I can make myself seem. My wrists are padded just enough to keep the circulation from being cut off. I could thrash and kick—I fought off rape a time or two in the army before I got to Sgt. Rae's squad, where you'd better believe no woman ever had to fear attack by fellow soldiers—but now I'm sinking into sub space, wide open, vulnerable.

"What's got into you, Specialist? What do you think you want?"

She knows, of course. By now we know almost everything about each other. My face is level with hers, a rare treat, and I try to focus on her face through my fog of obsession. The hair that was mostly dark two years ago is more salt than pepper now, and brush-cut shorter. There are lines around her eyes from more than the desert sun. The squareness of her face, so like her father's, is softened just enough by the graceful curve of her cheeks that I want to stroke it with my fingers and then my tongue, if I could only earn that privilege.

Sgt. Rae shifts so that her weight is mostly on the crossbar and slides one hand free of its ring. "Speak up, Brown!" She grabs my brown ponytail, yanks me close, and then shoves me away so that I spin one way and then the other as the ropes twist, untwist and twist again. When I sway close enough she swats me across my ass, or as close as she can reach, and I feel it all the way down my buttcheeks and between my thighs. She does it again, and then again, until the heat flows so deep inside me I think I might explode.

With all her weight on the crossbar through her chest and armpits, she reaches out to grip me by the shoulders, hard, hurting me just the way I like it. Then her big hands slide under my armpits so she's partly holding me up. My upstretched arms raise my small breasts. She rubs her thumbs across my nipples so hard and fast they must be standing out like bullets, and when she pinches them, sharp pangs of pleasure shoot down through my belly.

She knows where the worst of my scars are and works around them down my sides and ribs, trying not to be too rough even when I squirm and squeal and try to get even harder pressure from her fingers. I'm not silent any longer. It doesn't matter how I sound, what's pain and what's pleasure. All that matters is getting more and more.

Sgt. Rae's the one who has to use her safeword first. "At ease, Brown!" She grips the rings again and sinks slowly back into her chair.

My feet touch the ground. My arms drop, and I loosen the rope loops with my teeth, getting free just in time for her next order.

"Get over here, Jenny, stat!"

So I leap to straddle her lap, and she lifts me tight against her shoulder, right where I belong. Her free hand kneads my butt hard enough to make my cunt grind into her. I could come from that alone, but she needs more, more of my skin and heat and wetness, so she gets my pants down and sighs approval when I'm slippery enough for her calloused fingers to move easily between my folds. Back and forth, teasing, pressing deeper, a knuckle nudging my clit on each forward stroke. I want it all now, now! But I have to wait for her to drive me even harder, higher. This isn't just for me.

"Now." Rae's voice is strained. "Feel it. For both of us." I'm rocking with her thrusts, howling with need, taking everything she can fit inside me, and when the pleasure bursts through all control, I shout my joy to the treetops loud enough for two hearts, two bodies.

She holds me tight while my breathing slows toward normal. When I raise my head I see a tear trickling down her cheek. This doesn't scare me the way it used to. I've figured out that it's her own release of tension after she's made me feel what she can't feel anymore except through me. Being strong when that's what I need makes it safe to be vulnerable afterward. Besides, now's my chance to lick the tear away, kiss my way all across the face I love, ending with the lips that say more this way than words ever could.

Rae sets me gently away sooner, though, than usual. "Jenny,

there's something... Well, something that needs saying."

Now I'm scared. Hasn't everything already been said?

"You gave me back my life," she says, and pauses to search for the right words. "And I know you think I saved yours. So you could say there's no owing anything on either side."

I couldn't say that at all, so I just look at her. She sees my expression and strokes my face with such tenderness that fear melts away.

"I didn't mean... It's just that whatever we do, it's by choice. Maggie Burnside stopped by my desk today and asked, out of the blue, when we were going to get around to making things legal."

"Maggie the town clerk? Old Maggie Graniteside?"

"She's not so bad when you get to know her. And I guess she's come around to thinking we're not so bad, either. Or maybe she's decided to catch up with the twenty-first century without being dragged there."

"So what did you tell her?" I snuggle back against her side.

"I said the piece of paper might be nice to have, but it couldn't make us any closer, so I'd just go home and ask my wife."

"We might as well humor her, then. Set a good example." There'll be more to say later, and plenty of time to say it. Now, with the afterglow of lovemaking intensified by the hum of the motor, we don't need words at all as the mini-tank I built carries Sgt. Rae, and Sgt. Rae carries me home.

THE LONELIEST ROAD

Anna Meadows

Lila had thought of burning them. She'd even struck the match and held it so close that the blush-colored satin had begun to smoke. Then, just before the flame caught, she blew it out, leaving a dark spot on the fabric no bigger than a cigarette burn.

It had taken weeks to break them in. She had even slept with them folded under the mattress to soften the shank. Now she couldn't watch the stitched leather of the sole crumble to ash or the ribbons blacken and curl, even though they had been the ones she'd worn when that first pain had spread through her arches like glass shards through water.

She had always known she would never be a principal ballerina. She'd started too late, been too old by the time she got *en pointe*. Her shape was wrong, too short, her center of gravity a bit too low. Even when she survived on a poached egg in the morning and a handful of grapes at night, her ass stayed as full as twinned cherries, just like her mother's and her *abuela*'s. Only by the line of her arabesque and the beauty of her arches—"High as

God's saints and angels," her teacher had bragged to the artistic director—had she been accepted into her hometown's company, the smallest in Nevada.

None of it bothered her. She was happy to dance as one of a half dozen sugar plum fairies or tulle-skirted swans, grateful when cast as a nameless wood nymph in *La Sylphide*. She had never reached for the role of Juliet or *La Bayadère*.

This settling had protected her from jealousy. She congratulated lead dancers, who curled her hair and brushed glitter on her eyelids on opening nights. It had protected her from disappointment. Each time the costumer fitted her for the ensemble, she liked the feeling of the tape measure on her waist. But it hadn't protected her from the sense of glass in her muscles, so sudden and strong it took her from *elevé* to the stage floor, her rehearsal skirt floating like a jellyfish as she fell.

Six damning words came first from the ballet company specialist, with something like them repeated by a kinesiologist, a chiropractor, an orthopedist. A second opinion, a third, then, finally, the fourth, who told her to stop spending her money, that no doctor worth the co-pay would tell her anything different.

If you dance, you won't walk.

The same arches that had impressed the artistic director had weakened under years of *fouettés en tournant*. The pain, the wearing down of her tendons, would get worse with every adagio and *changement*. Even wanting to be one of many, a nameless sylph, was wanting too much.

It was her mother who told her to bring her *pointe* shoes to the tree out on Highway 50. "You can leave them, *m'ija*," her mother told her. "You will never see them, but you will know they are there." A cottonwood with a root system as big as a double-wide, the Middlegate tree sagged from the weight of hundreds of pairs of sneakers, oxfords, and dress shoes.

Converse hi-tops. Cross trainers and construction boots. Even a few children's jelly sandals, bright as Easter eggs, the straps of one attached to the buckle of the other.

If it had laces, or anything that could fasten one shoe to the other, someone had thrown it at that tree, the pair catching and hanging like the branches were telephone lines. The tree loomed above Lila, the shoes thick as greenery on the now fall-bare tree. Only a few leaves still clung between the laces.

A car or shipping truck flew down the highway once every five or ten minutes. There was nothing out here but sagebrush and desert in every direction. There was a reason they called US-50 the Loneliest Road in America.

The wind picked up, and a few cottonwood leaves tore away and drifted toward the highway. The pairs swayed in the wind, the toes of some kicking the sidewalls of others. No *pointe* shoes that Lila could see. She took them from her purse anyway, tying the ribbons of the left slipper to the ones of the right. Double-knot. A bow wouldn't hold, never had.

A few wisps escaped her neat bun. This morning, out of habit, she had gathered her hair back and pinned it in place.

A rusted-out Chevy pulled off the highway and parked a car's length behind Lila's '81 diesel. Lila wished she'd already thrown her *pointe* shoes over a branch. A tourist might spend a good fifteen minutes or half hour snapping pictures, and Lila didn't feel like small talk. She wanted the chance to do this alone, in the quiet she couldn't find anywhere else but the middle of Nevada, with no witnesses but a few donkey colts roaming the land on the other side of the two-lane.

The truck door opened, the woman stepping down from the cab in one certain motion. She wore what looked like men's Levi's and a white undershirt, short-sleeved, also a man's. Odd, given the temperature. Fifty-five when Lila had gotten out of her car, and it had to be cooler now that the sun had fallen low enough to splash amber along the horizon. Even in her ballet sweater, Lila shivered whenever the wind swept through the tree branches. The loose-knit ties, looped into a bow, fluttered just below her rib cage.

The muscles in the woman's arm showed as she threw the truck door shut. Lila put that together with something about her bearing and the way she squared her shoulders. Marine Corps. The woman had a sticker of the insignia on her back bumper, but Lila didn't need it. That stance was the same one her brother had brought home from recruit training. After that, Lila could always tell. It was something about the posture, I-beam-straight, and the way they set their chins.

If the way she stood and her bumper sticker weren't enough to make Lila sure, the woman had her straw-colored hair twisted into a bun at the nape of her neck, lower and tighter than Lila's. Her part was as sharp and straight as the metal edge on a wooden ruler. She and Lila wore the same hairstyle in name only. This woman's dress-code bun was as far from Lila's ballet chignon as her blond hair was from Lila's black.

The woman caught Lila staring and gave a nod of greeting, quick but polite. Lila tamped down her irritation. If this woman who had signed over her life to the USMC wanted to take a few pictures at the Middlegate shoetree, the least Lila could do was pull back onto the highway and leave her alone. Her *pointe* shoes could wait.

Then the women winked a slate blue eye at Lila, and Lila felt her cheeks flush to the color of her ballet slippers. Maybe she shouldn't leave. Maybe she should offer to get a shot of the woman standing in front of the cottonwood with all the swinging pairs in the background. Lila would want any other girl to do the same for her brother. She'd want her to take his picture. She'd want her to smile when he winked at her.

But there was no camera in the woman's hand, only a pair of worn combat boots. Sand-colored, Marine-issue. Her brother had come home wearing the same pair, identical in all but size.

Lila felt the veins in her chest wrapping around her heart. The woman had already tied the combat boots together. Their weight hung from her hand, the knotted laces wearing ruts in her fingers. Her eyes had the wet look of newly blown glass that had yet to cool and harden.

Lila looked for a limp or a few missing fingers, knowing she wouldn't find any. The military discharged women whose undershirts were just one of many things they had in common with men. This woman had come here for the same reason Lila had, to cast off shoes she no longer needed. Lila wondered if she hadn't gotten around to scratching the insignia off her bumper, or if she never would.

They both stood at the base of the tree, looking up into the ornamented branches. Neither Lila nor the woman drew her arms back to throw her shoes. The woman held on to the laces of her combat boots. Lila clutched the satin ribbons of the slippers she would never dance in again.

Lila wept into the sage-scented wind. The woman looked at her with a man's wince of not knowing what to do when a girl cries. She offered Lila the white square of a clean handkerchief. Lila nodded her thanks, her tears soaking the thin cotton. The woman's eyes still looked wet as new glass, but she did not cry.

Lila cried for her. The desert opened and accepted the sound, carrying it over the salt flats. The sun had fallen below the horizon when they both slumped away from the tree. The woman nodded at the cottonwood, conceding the fight. Lila turned her back to the broad trunk, her *pointe* shoe ribbons still twirling on her fingers. They were still beautiful, even if she couldn't use them anymore. The satin matched the tea roses that grew in her grandmother's side yard. She had crossed and tied the ribbons over her ankles so many times that they were softest at the center of the knot. She'd traced her fingers over the binding and vamp so many times that the oil of her hands left them shined. The fabric on the toe had almost worn through to the box from countless *relevés*.

The woman grabbed Lila's hand just before her fingers reached the car door. Lila started, her eyes flashing up to the woman's face. The woman slowly reached out her other hand toward Lila, her combat boots still hanging from her fingers. Lila accepted their weight, her fingers brushing the woman's as the laces slid from one palm to the other.

The satin of the *pointe* shoe ribbons slipped from Lila's fingers. She stepped back, thinking she'd dropped them, but then saw them cradled in the woman's hand. Now Lila understood the trade, the handing off. It was easier to let someone else do it. They turned back to the tree, swung their arms back, and let go.

Both combat boots and *pointe* shoes arced through the air, the worn laces and satin ribbons crossing and tangling as they caught on an open branch. The moment of sand-brown and the shine of pink satin in the last of the daylight broke Lila open. She pressed her lips to the woman's, the sound of her sobbing filling both their mouths. The woman only kissed her back, her mouth as chapped and dry as the cracked ground of the Nevada desert.

Lila pulled away just enough to speak, their foreheads still touching. "Thank you," she said, though for what she didn't know. For being willing to die for her and everybody else, even those who'd sent her away with nothing but those combat boots. For keeping a hand on the small of Lila's back, a palm's width of warmth for when winter settled over the Great Basin.

The woman answered by pulling the pins from Lila's hair until it fell loose, and guiding Lila's hand to the back of her neck, an invitation to do the same. Lila found the last pin just in time for the wind to pick up, the sudden gust intertwining the strands, countless wheat-colored laces and dark ribbons.

THE CHERRY STEM

Diane Woodrow

She thinks I don't remember, but I do. I can still see her doing that thing to the cherry stem with her lips and her tongue the first time we ever met—somehow tying it in a knot. I got wet just thinking about how that tongue would feel on me, in me, making me shiver, making me come.

Twenty years and two kids—twins—later, I still see that cherry stem, and I still want that tongue. There's almost too much between us now, though. Kids are the least of it. Jobs, parents who aren't, really, anymore, and the fond—but indistinct—attachment that two lovers share after they've been together for so long.

Sometimes it would be easier if we hadn't been with each other—at each other—for the last twenty years. I know all her secrets now, or at least I think I do, and she thinks she knows mine. After the kids were born, there wasn't much time for anything except them and their relentless need. Our life got shoved somewhere else for a while.

If I tell the truth to myself, though, it had been shoved somewhere else long before that. She was on the road most of the week, and I was struggling to get an education and get a new business off the ground. We never seemed to catch each other at a good time—any time really.

Like two ships—ah, but that's cliché. It was really emotional distance that seeped in and grew into some sort of maw that swallowed us both up in a cruelly quotidian ennui.

Growing apart just doesn't seem to describe it. We didn't grow, precisely, as much as we just wandered. Now, as I look over at her when she's working or surfing the Net—I can't tell which anymore—I still see that cherry stem and wonder what it might be like to feel that tongue.

I still love her, and she tells me she still loves me, but in between school plays and hockey and sitting with Mom because she can't be alone anymore at age eighty-four, the passion has left for decidedly more fertile grounds. It was starving here.

Sometimes I wonder what it would take to get us back to that first night. We'd had a rocky dating relationship—if you could call it that—and we were sitting in my car watching the cold rain run in abstract rivulets down the windows, shielding us from the outside and prying eyes. She looked over at me and asked, "What's on your mind?"

I almost laughed out loud. "You!" I wanted to scream, as if she didn't know, couldn't tell that my heart was jerking uncontrollably and my senses were threatening to desert me. I could see the swell of her chest as she breathed, fogging up the windows, and I wanted so much to touch her, to feel her, to be that cherry stem.

I chickened out. "What do you want?" I challenged her, hoping she'd tell me it was me. She sighed and looked down, trying to pick invisible lint off her pants. "I don't know. There's Lindy."

"Fuck Lindy!" I snarled. "Didn't you leave her, that, in Austin?"

She made some sort of little choking sound that tore at me, flaying me open. "Yes." It was a whisper laced with pain.

"Well, then, what's the problem?" I was just young and stupid enough to believe that if I loved her, I could help her forget that her heart had just been handed back to her in a body bag.

"I don't want to be hurt again." Again, that pain coming from somewhere I couldn't touch, couldn't heal.

I sat silent for a long time, not knowing what to say. I was twenty-five and not very experienced—especially with women and their ability to totally lacerate my self-control and my heart at the same time.

There had been a couple of straight girls—one of whom I had loved and the other whom I had fucked. Then there was the first real girlfriend. None of them had really taken my heart for the ride that this one had. I was totally out of control and had no idea how to get it back.

She sat for a long time and then sighed from somewhere deep down. "If you could be anywhere in the world right now, where would you be?"

I looked at her with all the juvenile intensity I could brandish, desire coiling in my belly like a copperhead. "Alone with you, in a bed, fucking you." I waited for her to laugh or to run, assuming the equal possibility of both.

I got neither. "What are you waiting for?" Her eyes were on me, inside me, taunting me, humor and need swirling dangerously through the green flecked with fiery hazel.

I didn't say much. I couldn't, really. I just put the car in gear and headed for home. My home. My bed. Before we got up to my room, we were at each other, clothes flying and buttons ripping and pinging off the floor like shards of glass.

The tongue was just as good as advertised by the cherry stem. So were the hands. I lost track of how many times she made me come. When it was over, I knew it was too late to go back, and so did she. From then on, we were together.

That was nineteen years and three months ago. Now it's different. We're different. I'm not fat, but I am cuddly, and she's always somewhere else, even when she's here with me. When I touch her, she doesn't shiver anymore; sometimes she pulls away.

I ask what's wrong, but she always mutters that she doesn't feel good about herself, her body. It strains my patience, since I think she's gorgeous—more now at forty-five than she was at twenty-five. There's a toughness to her now that wasn't there before, and that's so sexy. She doesn't know that because I don't tell her. I don't think it's important anymore to tell her.

I've stopped trying to talk about it. It hasn't done anything but frustrate us both. She hoards words like gold, too precious to spend. I babble on, trying to find the one word that will penetrate her barriers, and so it goes, back and forth, this demented game of sound and silence, until we're spent and angry. It's not worth it.

One night at dinner, as I'm trying to dodge flying peas, trying to get the pie ready for dessert, I look up and catch her staring. I can see it in her eyes, that raw, naked want that makes my insides go mushy and my knees wobble. I haven't seen that in a very long time—maybe two years—and my breath catches. She just smiles. *Maybe*, I think cautiously, *she's back.*

I return the look, and she catches it. We've uncertainly rewired a connection that I thought might have been lost. It feels…strange. Funny how you can look at your wife, your lover, of twenty years and feel that way, as if seeing desire in her eyes is odd, but it is. And exhilarating. It's been so long since I've felt that rush of blood between my legs—for her anyway. I've had needs, and I've taken care of them by myself.

Now we're throwing looks at each other across the dinner table like two fifteen-year-olds trying to flirt and keep Daddy from noticing it. Only in our case, it's two six-year-olds who we need to keep oblivious. I'm also still trying to figure out whether or not this is an aberration of some kind. Is she drunk? Is she guilty of something? It's uneven ground that I'm afraid to tread.

There's something to be said for not being able to act on your impulses right away. It heightens the need to fulfill them, mercilessly. Right after dinner, there's hockey practice. Then it's bath time and bedtime and time for all the other rituals that make up coziness. Sex doesn't really enter that picture.

I'm tired, so I go to bed. We keep odd hours because it seems she never has the need to sleep. Sometime during the night, I feel her slip into the bed. I want to roll over and touch her, but I don't. There's school and work and the thousand other things that have to be done, so sleep is a precious commodity.

I do dream, though. She's on me, in me, fingers probing, curling, diving through the slick-hot wetness between my legs. My hips rise to meet her thrusts, and I cry out, needing to come. She knows just how to work me, too, and I shudder over and over again. I wake up in a sweat, the last tendrils of the orgasm still flowing through me, mocking me. "Damn."

I'm ill-tempered all day. The kids can't do anything right, and my coworkers cast surreptitious glances at me, as though they're wary that I might uncoil and bite them. My daughter looks at me and rolls her eyes. I know she thinks I'm crazy. She can perceive my moods, even at six. Both kids leave me alone. I'm grateful, because how do you explain this kind of maddening frustration to kids?

I don't get any more hot looks over the dinner table either, and that pisses me off even more. I don't stop to consider that my general bitchiness may be chasing them away. Instead I clank dishes in the sink like a petulant child. I can't even name what I want, but it isn't this now-severed connection.

The next few days drag by and I start to think that the come-fuck-me look was a dream just like the wet one that I had. Then, while I'm bent over plucking weeds from my hens and chicks, I feel heat on me and I flush.

Looking up, I see her staring at me like she could eat me, and like that's exactly what she's going to do. The blood leaves my head and goes straight between my legs, momentarily robbing me of the ability to think or speak. I'm standing there like an idiot with something between a scowl and a grin plastered to my sweaty, dirty face.

"What?" I manage, when I can make my tongue work again.

"Nothing!" she snaps sharply, looking guilty like I've caught her five-fingering swag at the dime store. She turns and tramps off, leaving me breathless and confused.

Another couple of days go by, and I'm beginning to feel as if I've landed in some sort of altered universe. One minute, I'll catch her staring at me, her need simmering in her eyes, and the next, she's got her head buried in a book, oblivious to me and anything else.

It was better when there was no possibility of contact. We just went on with our routines, comfortable in the familiarity that twenty years breeds. If the sex was gone, the love wasn't and that seemed like enough.

Now it doesn't. I'm trying to figure out what's going on, but communication is a two-way street. I can ask, but she doesn't answer—either because she doesn't have any, or because she doesn't want to. Either way, I feel like I'm one of those bolo paddle balls—jerked around on a string and constantly banging my head, trying to find some sort of equilibrium that won't come.

Sometimes the glances are so forceful, I can feel them on me as if they were her hands or tongue, searing me with the heat of her want. I'm either perpetually wet or annoyed these days, and it's beginning to fray my nerves—which, with six-year-old twins, aren't that strongly lashed together to begin with. All I want is an explanation.

It doesn't seem to be forthcoming either. I try coming on to her—clumsily, because that's all I can manage—but it doesn't work. She smiles, but she's firmly established the distance between us, and the only way it can be bridged is when she chooses to favor me with one of those heat-seeking looks that both melts and vexes me.

Then the touches start. About a month after the flying-pea exchange, she comes up behind me and starts to massage my shoulders. It's not like she hasn't done this hundreds of times over the last twenty years.

She never quit touching me really, but these are *touches*—the ones where the sexual energy is taut, like the hairs on the back of your neck when you hear a strange sound alone at night.

Her hands quit my shoulders and sensuously travel the length of my arms, leaving fire and need along her fingertips' path. I moan involuntarily and lean back into her. When I do, she slips away, leaving me alone and excruciatingly aroused, my clit hard and throbbing. "Damn it!" I mutter, my insides twisted with want.

The next night, I'm maudlin, so I listen to the Indigo Girls—*Rites of Passage*—as I do the dishes. It's what we fell in love to, and it reminds me of why I'm still here. The soaring, anguished words talk to me, telling me that someone else feels this choking need and anger.

I'm lost in the music when I feel her hands slip around me

from behind. I freeze like I would if I saw a fawn in the yard, afraid that the least little move would scare it away. Even my breath stops for a moment.

She works her hands upward in a slow, agonizing motion toward my breasts. I ache for her to touch them, squeeze them, move the nipples around between her fingers and thumbs, replace those hands with her tongue. A groan escapes me, and I'm embarrassed. Her voice, low and dulcet in my ear, stops my breath again. "Hey, there." The words are a delicious frisson down my spine.

My breath is coming in short, ragged pants now, and my chest is heaving. My knees threaten to liquefy. All I can do is groan. The ability to utter words seems to have left me.

She squeezes again and laughs, a melody like bells jingling on a sleigh in winter, sharp and promising. "What's wrong?" she purrs, as if she doesn't know that I can barely stand. Her hand travels down my abdomen and up under my shirt. As her fingers tease and tighten my nipples, I gasp at the pleasure. It's been so long.

Like the other night, before I can adjust to this newness, she's gone again, but things have changed. We're talking again, and the computer is mostly off at night after the kids are in bed. The conversations are just that—actual grown-up topics that don't revolve around schedules and playdates and doctors' appointments for Mom. We talk politics—my favorite—and football (hers).

She smiles more easily now, and so do I. If this is an alternate universe, I wouldn't mind sticking around for a while. Its language and customs are much sweeter than in my own. I'm not pushing, though. I get the impression that any wrong move will send her scrambling for cover.

"How about a date?" she says out of the blue one Saturday

morning at hockey practice, while the boy is doing puck drills and the girl is off playing with her friends at the other end of the rink—still in visual range.

"As in a date night?" I venture, unsure of myself.

"Yes." I can see the…something…dancing in her eyes. It stirs me, and I return the gaze. She gets the message and reaches over and takes my hand in both of hers, gently massaging the top of it, taking my breath away. I don't move for fear of breaking the spell. The simple touch is racing through me, and it's hard to think straight. All I do is feel, and it's so good.

As the week goes on, I'm on pins and needles. Anticipation makes it so much sweeter. I wonder if she can sense it as the adrenaline courses through me at her touch—which, by the way, is happening more frequently these days. Desire flows through me like quicksilver, heating my blood.

Finally. Friday night is here. I'm surprised, and a little confused, when she comes home early and scoops up the kids and heads for the front door. "Where's the sitter?"

"They're spending the night at Deb's." Her eyes are molten; all the hazel is gone, replaced by emerald on fire. With that, she's out the door and back before I can even get dressed.

The dinner is excellent—both the food and the company. As I look at her across the candlelit table, I realize that not only have I never stopped loving her, I've never stopped lusting after her either.

She's sexy tonight in a way I haven't seen in a long time, maybe ever. Her hair is longer now, and it flows richly around her shoulders, like dark chocolate from a fountain. She's wearing girly clothes, too—a silent concession to me—and they accentuate her lithe body and make it look…yummy.

She sees me blush. "What?" A small smile sneaks up on her lips, curling them deliciously.

Cat's got my tongue. I blush some more, and my face is on fire now. "It's just…" I can't get the words out, so I let my eyes talk, and I'm pretty sure she gets the message.

When the waiter comes for the drink order, I get my usual—a Sam Light.

"Tom Collins," she says, with a lilt to her voice that I don't quite get.

The drinks arrive, and I finally get it. Atop the frosted glass sits a cherry with a very long stem. I blush again, and this time she smiles at me, a wicked look that makes my belly flare with fire.

Deliberately, agonizingly, she pops the cherry into her mouth and chews. Even that's sexy.

Then there's no cherry, only the stem. Her lips, lush and sensuous, worry it around, and her tongue darts out now and then in a luscious, languorous dance. I'm mesmerized, and my eyes grow hazy with something I can only describe as wanton lust.

I'm barely breathing as I watch the play of her tongue and lips. My mouth waters and my hands clench and unclench, craving…something. She's watching me as she works the cherry, enjoying this, enjoying seeing me squirm with need.

Finally, she's done, and the cherry stem is tied in a perfect knot, along with my stomach. I fix her with a look that screams with yearning, and she returns it, leaving me breathless and nearly senseless.

She looks at me with a mischievous smirk. "If you could be anywhere in the world right now, where would you be?"

My reply is automatic. I've finally found the words I need, though I don't recognize the rasping voice that says them. "Alone with you, in a bed, fucking you."

"Let's go." Her voice is thick with excitement and need that burns me to my very soul.

I don't ask where we're going. I don't care. My mind isn't

functioning nearly as well as my...other parts. She's silent, too, intent on the destination, but she reaches over and strokes my hand with a lover's caress. I am so wet and ready, and I wonder if she can tell.

We're there, finally. It's the swanky hotel by the river that runs through the city. I've never been here, and I should take the time to take it in, but I don't. My only focus is on getting to the room—alone with her.

As soon as the door clicks shut, she's on me, hands every-where at once, making me hot and shivering at the same time. I can't breathe, and the walls are closing in. I fist my fingers in her hair, throw my head back and let it take me.

Somehow, we make it to the bed and she's on top of me. Her hands are shaking. "God, I need you!" she growls like a beau-tiful, wild animal that's come to devour me.

"Uh. Oh. God. Yes," is all I can say through the haze of sensations that are relentlessly assaulting me, body and soul.

She kisses that little hollow at the base of my throat and draws the skin in, biting and leaving a mark. I arch off the bed to preserve the contact. She nips again and moves lower.

Suddenly, my nipple is in her mouth, and she's sucking it, none too gently. I scream out—for an instant embarrassed that someone might hear. Then, as she flicks it with her tongue, I don't care anymore. Again, I lose myself.

Lower she goes, until she's making languorous circles on my stomach with her tongue, slowly converging on the center—my center. It's pounding, and I raise my hips, desperately begging for her.

I hear a growl, and I look up, finding her eyes. They're almost black with desire, and it sends a river of fire raging through me. I'm blind with need, unthinking, and almost unconscious. I push her shoulders down, boldly asserting my need.

She laughs, a low, naughty sound that makes the fire burn impossibly hotter and higher.

"Please," I beg. "Suck me."

She does. As she parts my legs, then my lips, I nearly explode and desperately try to hold back, wanting this never to end, but knowing that if she keeps touching me this way, it will, all too soon.

Her tongue is on me then, turning me molten, making me ache with delicious pleasure-pain. I can't see, I can't think. I can only feel. Her lips, sucking me, drawing the blood down, causing me to stiffen, to pulse, to throb, to crave release. Ah, so good!

Suddenly it's on me, the first waves unwinding and trailing down my thighs and up my spine. Delicious spasms of sheer bliss. The tendrils of the orgasm uncoil, releasing their fire in paroxysms of ecstasy.

I curl forward, shuddering violently, fisting my hands in her hair to hold that wonderful tongue in place. "I'm coming!" It's a ragged gasp, torn from my throat, pleasure so pure it's near agony.

As I lie in the after—that sweet semi-sleep-wakefulness—I murmur to her incoherently, not understanding, not thinking, only feeling the last gentle waves and lassitude that come with sweet satisfaction.

She moves up and caresses my face. "So, was it worth the wait?"

I can hear the gentle humor, and it warms me.

My hips move languidly against her, wanting more but not being able to take it just yet. "Yes. Absolutely." My words are slurred, drunk with the decadence of it all.

For a while, we just lie together. After a time, I can talk again, and I look up to catch her eye. "That was the longest seduction in history," I whisper, still unable to speak quite normally. "Where did it come from?"

Her answer surprises me, because I think she doesn't remember. "You remember the night you made cherry pie?"

I get it now. I'm the cherry stem.

LIFE DRAWING

Catherine Paulssen

The room does nothing to reflect my excitement. It's a plain community college classroom, its walls painted light yellow—years ago, obviously, for the paint has cracked and looks faded in the unflattering light shining down from the tubular lamps. But this does nothing to diminish the happy agitation fluttering in my belly as I put my bag down on one of the chairs arranged in a half circle around a curved lounger and take a look at the other students scattered across the room—some chattering, some positioning their drawing boards and supplies.

I've finally overcome my anxiety and signed up for a nude drawing class.

I'm not the model, mind you.

Nevertheless, drawing a naked person is something I've shied away from for several reasons. For one thing, it takes great skill. What if I'm not good at it? What if I don't get the proportions right? I would have to face the fact that I'm not as talented as people around me like to make me believe. My favorite pastime, and maybe something I could do professionally at some point in my life, would be tainted.

And then, of course, it's so personal.

I take a peek around the room and wonder if the model is already among the ten or twelve people milling around me. Let's hope it's not the old guy with the sagging chin and sunken shoulders. I'm not so keen on seeing him naked.

My eyes wander to a girl about my age. She wears a gray bolero jacket over a tank top. I like how the olive skin above her armpit shows when she wraps a hairband around her long, golden brown tresses or plants her hands on her hips. Her butt is round, hugged nicely by a pair of tight dark jeans. The fluttering in my stomach gets a little stronger.

A breeze from the door makes me turn. In walks a tall woman in her early fifties. She has a square face and hawk-like nose. Behind her is a girl wearing a pink wraparound cardigan and a light green skirt. Even the freckles on her skin are pale. If she were a palette, she'd be all shades of pastel. And yet, the way she moves is more graceful than fragile. Like a ballet dancer. The really good ones look so effortless you almost forget how strong they are, how many hours of practice they've logged.

"Welcome," the tall woman says.

There's some noise as people sit down and shove their bags underneath chairs. Eventually, everyone looks at her with mixed expressions.

"Welcome to my class," she says. "I'm Rose." Her eyes, which she turns to the dainty girl by her side, are friendly behind her rimless glasses. "This is my godchild, Joni. She's been kind enough to agree to serve as our model for the upcoming weeks."

Joni gives a reserved smile as everyone in the semicircle mumbles some hello, and I can tell she hasn't been a nude model for such a big group before. For a moment, our eyes lock and she holds my gaze. Her eyes are as round as her face.

Joni vanishes behind a folding screen, and Rose starts introductions. I barely pay attention. My mind is busy picturing Joni stepping out of her skirt. Loosening that wraparound sweater. I bet she's wearing matching bra and underwear. White with some sort of pattern. Little dots. Light-colored flowers. For a moment, I entertain myself picturing her covered with tattoos, the J.Crew getup just a cover.

I clear my throat and force myself to listen to the other students introduce themselves. Kenneth: blond, tall, college-student poster boy. The old guy's name is Marlon. Cute Butt is Jessie. Next to me sits a dark-haired, nervous guy who introduces himself with a Greek accent. His name's Stani, and he's taking this class as preparation to enroll at UCLA.

Rose turns her gaze to me.

"I'm Audra," I say. "Um...I'm twenty-eight, from Silver Lake, and I'm trying to find out if I can become better skilled in what I've been doing so far."

That moment, Joni steps from behind the curtain. If ever a painter has been looking for inspiration to paint his version of the foam-risen goddess, here she is. Stani next to me fumbles with his eraser. It falls down, and I'm glad for the little commotion he causes as he dives for it and then hits his head on my elbow.

Joni lowers her head. I think she's hiding a smile, but her right hand still plays nervously with the forefinger of her other hand. Only now do I notice the small silver band around her ring finger. Of course. Somebody else already saw the obvious.

Rose directs her onto the lounger, and as Joni's hourglass-shaped figure molds into the chaise's tightly curled wave— her head propped on one arm, her other arm resting on her delicately curved thigh—I'm thankful that Rose gives instructions for what to do.

"Start simple," she tells us. "Try to catch the body's shape. Study its silhouette. Don't focus on details at this point, and don't do a portrait."

I rub my hands against my jeans and open my sketch block. I draft a few lines on the paper, add a few more, then find myself staring into her eyes again. My palms grow hot. Sleek, shoulder length chestnut hair frames her face. Her forehead is covered by straight bangs. She has the face of a porcelain doll. Not the aloof kind, more like a pin-up version. Cute rather than sophisticated. Too bad we're not supposed to focus on the head. I could do a whole study of those pale blue eyes and the little dimple underneath her mouth. Or run my fingers across it.

Joni blushes, but I'm the one who looks away. I clutch the pencil a bit tighter as my stare wanders down her body. Her breasts rest comfortably on her tummy. The nipples are dark against her creamy complexion. There's a little birthmark on the upper left side of her breast, a perfect brown dot. There's another, bigger one right above the hairline of her delta. My gaze wanders over the wispy tuft of hair between her legs, then down her thighs to the pit of her knees, landing, finally, at her feet. Her toenails are painted coral pink, but they've already grown out a bit—not so much that it looks sloppy, but enough to tell she applied the polish a while ago. The lacquer is completely chipped on one of her left toes.

As my pencil follows the journey of my eyes, I wondered if you could capture affection on paper?

While lying on the thinly upholstered lounger—I really need to ask Rose to bring some cushions next week—I watch the faces of people sitting around, watching me. It's not my first time posing as a nude model, but so far, I've mostly done it for people I know. It's different to undress in front of strangers, and I don't like it. There are the ones who gawp. They try to hide it, but I can still see it in their eyes. There are the ones who, after two or three sessions, think they know you. They've seen you naked. They've seen you in poses familiar from their favorite paintings by some Renaissance artist, and so you become *their* bathing Virgin. They study every wrinkle, every nook of your body, and mistake that for what lies beneath. The mixture of adulation and faux intimacy makes them bold enough to ask you out. You always say no.

If my mom's best friend hadn't been so persuasive—and if she wasn't my godmother—I wouldn't be here anyway. But maybe this time I need to thank her for her persistence. That girl that introduced herself as Audra has a wonderful voice. Deep, soothing. And also raw. It's a bit gravelly. Maybe she's a smoker? I'd like to hear more of that voice.

Over her drawing board, she throws a glance at me, and another. A longer one, followed by a shy peek. As if she's confirming something. Her eyes are dark brown with freckles in them that shine warmly even in the bright sunlight streaming in through the huge windows.

It's been a long time since someone has looked at me that way.

When I enter the classroom the following week, I'm even more excited than the first time. I hum that song about Bette Davis's eyes to calm myself down. Actually, it hasn't left my head all week. Joni's already there, and I catch her stare as she sits down on the lounger, dressed in nothing but a short robe. Not a robe per se. More like a short, very sexy version of a kimono. She gives me a smile, and I quickly avert my eyes.

* * *

Rose has just announced the break when everyone is already up and out of the classroom. The chilly conditioned air has percolated into each pore, and I wish I'd brought my snuggly terry-cloth bathrobe instead of this fancy satin thing. I stretch my limbs and feel Audra's eyes following my movement. I know it's shallow to flaunt this way. And yet I can't resist the temptation. Her stare is already making me feel warmer.

I wish the old guy wasn't staying. Why isn't he going to catch some air like everyone else? I wait a few moments. He's not going anywhere, so I slip into the bathrobe. Maybe it's pointless since she's seen all of me anyway, but I feel elegant in it. Attractive.

So she's not a smoker. She's not leaving, not even to get a coffee or some candy from the vending machine. Good thing I can't go for some candy in this state of semi-undress. I've gained seven pounds in the past two weeks. They say food can't compensate for love. I bet *they* never discovered their girlfriend is a cheater.

It's just me and Marlon left in the room—and Joni. I want to talk to her, but all the questions I come up with in my head sound so shallow. "So, modeling, huh?" I roll my eyes at my unspoken lameness and continue doodling. I blend the charcoal with my fingertips and add finishing touches to her knuckles. She has very giving hands. One look at them and you know they can make you feel better instantly on a bad day. I wonder if whoever gave her that ring knows how to reciprocate their warmth.

From memory, I start to draw her eyes. I avoid looking into them. I sigh, wishing I was bolder, wishing I knew what was going on behind those Bette Davis eyes. But I'm afraid of what they might see if I let them look at me closely.

My flow is interrupted by the beat coming out of Kenneth's earphones. He passes my chair, holding a huge sandwich and a cup of coffee. Joni's gaze follows him.

I get up so swiftly I almost knock over my chair. "Can I get you anything?" I ask, a bit embarrassed for all of us for forgetting she might be hungry.

Surprise lightens her face, and she smiles and shakes her head. "Thanks, I'm fine."

I turn my eyes to the old man, but he's so caught up in his sketches he doesn't even notice. Nevertheless, now I have to go get myself some snack. Damn it. I'd rather stay, now that I've finally managed to break the ice.

I'm late for the next class, but my apology gets stuck in my throat when I lay eyes upon the sight before me as I rush into the room and crash down onto the first empty seat. Joni is lying face-down on the lounger, her butt only scarcely covered by a silk shawl, one leg dangling on the side so that her foot grazes the floor, the other leg sprawled over the length of the cushions.

"Please stretch your hands over your head," Rose commands, "and place your wrists on the headrest. Hands on top of each other."

She moves Joni's hands a bit, and that's when I see it: a whitish patch of skin that circles her finger. The ring is gone. I lean back as much as I can to see what is visible of her face. She looks pallid, even by her standards, and she's not trying to hide her ashen complexion. She looks bare. Real. And abysmally lonely.

I see myself lying next to her. I wrap my arm around her and tell her how beautiful she is. I wait for the warmth of my skin to permeate hers and suck a little at her neck between whispers about anything and nothing at all. I look up and watch her eyes, willing the languor out of them before trailing kisses down her spine. My hand travels over her butt and between her cheeks down to the heated, moist lips covering the tender spot I'm aiming for. She buries her head in the cushion, smiling, moaning. She perks up her provocative butt and allows me to indulge her, and indulge in her too.

I shudder and look up, horrified. Did I let that noise out loud?

Holding one position for thirty minutes is difficult enough. But now, as a sudden breeze brushes my skin and I hear someone rush into the room, it becomes especially hard. I want to turn around. I want to confirm that the tingle trickling down the skin of my back, which has nothing to do with the whiff of air, really is a physical manifestation of my hope that it's Audra who's just entered. I want to know if I get to see her when I'm finally allowed to rise from the chaise and shake out my limbs. More importantly, I want to know if I will feel her stare on me later, feel the warm blanket of her gaze covering me.

Her eyes are radiant. But what makes them really special is the way they look at me. How they take me in and lift me up whenever she feels free to let them.

I crane my head as little as possible until, from the very corner of my eye, I finally see her. The tingle transforms into a snug, fuzzy feeling in my belly. I've spent the last days doing nothing but sleeping, watching TV, and crying. I haven't even bothered to shower or comb my hair or brush my teeth. Naturally, shopping for groceries was out of the question. I've turned instead to our—*my*—supply of canned peaches and tuna. The scary part is that living this way hasn't bothered me either. I couldn't drag myself out of bed anyway, not even for the rings of the phone or doorbell. I can't face them yet—my friends, with their gifts of sweets, chicken soup, ice cream and booze. Goodies meant to comfort my soul.

I wouldn't have broken that routine for anyone other than Audra. In retrospect, it doesn't seem so difficult to have gotten out of bed. Or maybe seeing Audra is making me feel that it wasn't. What was I mourning anyway? Beth's and my relationship had been dying for months.

I hear the drawing of a shivering breath, and it sends a chill up my spine. A thrill spreads between my legs. The hairs on my arm prickle, and now I know I'm wrapped up in her eyes.

I hope she doesn't notice the cellulite on my thighs. Of course, I know she will. This is really not the most flattering light, and I'm completely exposed. I hope she doesn't mind, at least. I would really love to see how she sees me. To see one of her sketches. I would love to know what's going through her head while she's drawing me. Is she really watching me, or does she merely see a body lying there, a challenge she has to overcome on her way to becoming a better artist? And even if she's only seeing me as a subject, does she like what she sees? Am I pretty in her eyes, maybe even sexy? I'm certain she's into girls. I've seen her checking out the brunette's ass. Can't blame her—that chick has a picture-perfect behind. Not like mine. I bet no cellulite mars her olive-colored skin. And she's always so well groomed with her stupid shiny hair and long lashes. I'm just a slump who's been two-timed by her girlfriend. The worthless lying bitch. And not even *she* was attracted to me anymore.

Next week, I'll be wearing makeup again.

Blood pulsing in my ears, I listen to the rustle of clothes behind the folding screen. Rose speaks slowly. There's always a break between her sentences, which are rather short. In those breaks, I can hear Joni undressing herself. I can't wait for the moment she steps in front of the class. Actually, I hate that there's a class. I hate the other students, I even hate Rose. I wish none of them were here. I wish none of them would get to see her, share in the moment of euphoria when she emerges. Their presence takes away from the silent understanding between us that I've been feeling lately.

I sigh and straighten up. Rose explains some principles for today's task. "You alienate the body. How you do that is up to you. Be creative. But stick to the basics I told you about."

Joni appears, and she's so perfect that the hollow yearning inside me grows larger, possesses more and more of me. The ring's still gone. But her eye shadow is back. And her toes are polished cherry red.

She takes a relaxed kneeling position on the lounger, gazing toward the window as though she were on a deserted beach, looking out for a ship to arrive. Her back is like a smooth, shimmering canvas.

I imagine sitting behind her, and she giggles when my brush touches her skin. I take a long sweep down her spine, coloring it in lush green. Her shoulder blades move as she suppresses her laughter, and she keeps complaining about how I tickle her. I admonish her for being so silly but secretly relish her sensitivity and the effect my touch has on her. When she doesn't let up, I lower the brush and lean in to whisper into her ear. I tell her that if this is all the titillation she can take, what will she do when I cover her breasts in hues of purple and violet? When I circle her nipple with a slim brush, dipped deeply into cold, creamy paste? She gasps and bites her lips. But she remains patient from now on. I give her a little kiss on the nape of her neck before adorning her body with dry deserts, muddy lakes, splashes of light, with the sun rising and the moon blinking in a snow-capped mountain, with carpets woven of leaves, blossoms, corn ears. I paint feathers on her skin, and fur, the coat of a leopard and the scales of a fish.

* * *

The sky outside the classroom window is bright and cloudless. The green slopes of the San Fernando Valley are met by the bare, jagged mountains in the distance, painted copper by the light of the setting sun. The air glistens in a colorless stripe where the sky meets their grayish tops and stretches out into the vast space.

I'd rather watch Audra. Or ask her to paint the sight for me. I'd hang it over my bedroom dresser and enjoy the beauty of it whenever I wanted. I'd tell people she drew it for me, and would be proud when I told them.

I wonder what she will draw me like? I know it's going to be good. I know she'll find a way to alienate my body and still make it prettier. When she was driving me home last week, Rose gushed on and on about how talented Audra was. But I don't need Rose to tell me. I took a peek at her papers during coffee break two weeks ago, when Audra was out of the room. She'd created some doodles that stunned me. There was a drawing of my hands that made them look as though they were caressing the paper. I've never thought about anyone seeing my hands—really *seeing* them. She made them look...almost generous. It sounds silly, doesn't it? I know. But I swear, that's how she captured them. And simply as a way to kill time during a coffee break.

When we're done with our studies, Rose collects the papers and pins them to the board. There are limbs out of proportion. There's a drawing of half a body and half a skeleton. There's a mermaid. There's something that looks as though a school child had been asked to imitate Picasso. There's a drawing of Joni with wings and eagle's claws and a tail. And there's mine. The world in Joni's body.

Rose picks the Picasso. "This is from you, Kenneth, right?" She looks at the drawing that shows Joni's breasts distorted, a grotesquely big butt, her one leg significantly shorter than the other, and the arms bulky and stumpy. "Would you explain why you chose this technique?"

Kenneth assumes an air of importance. "Because the body is flawed," he says without moving a muscle. "I wanted to show its imperfections."

Arrogant prick. I throw him a furious look, which Rose seems to pick up on. "Audra, your point of view is different?" she asks. "Which picture is yours—this?" She takes down my drawing and offers it to the class for a closer view. "The body, painted with flowers and animal skin and all sorts of geological patterns, eventually becomes a brook. Now what did you want to say with that—that the body dissolves? Is your painting an allegory for the circle of life?"

My outrage turns to shame. I feel the blood rush to my cheeks with unstoppable force. I can't possibly tell her that I painted what I did because that's what I'd like to paint on Joni's body, can I?

"I...I felt the only way to abstract the body was to turn it into a piece of art itself. I mean, it's so perfect already, the way it's created...uh... What I'm trying to say is..."

Joni tilts her brow. The edge of her mouth twitches.

"By turning the body itself into the artwork, I try to unite the viewer and the art through familiar patterns. Because we're part of nature, and...and nature's part of us, so...instead of alienating the body, we should learn to become one with the universe again...learn that every one of us encompasses a part of it..." I pause, realizing I'm babbling. And *such* bullshit.

Joni sucks her bottom lip into her mouth. I get the feeling that one look of those pale blue pools at my flushed cheeks is telling her more about my real thoughts than I'd like to reveal.

"Very well," says Rose, handing me back my drawing. "We'll

discuss the other pieces next week." I feel Stani's admiring look and hastily shove my things into my bag.

But when I get up to leave, Joni catches my eye. A glow softens her gaze. I don't hesitate. Maybe I should, but I don't. With a quick move, I fold the paper and press it into her hand. I don't wait for her to react. With a brief look into her astonished eyes, I turn and scurry out of the classroom.

When I return the following week, a thick wall of stifling air greets me as I enter the classroom. Stani fans himself with a piece of paper. Joni sits on the windowsill wearing her bathrobe, but even that seems like too much fabric in the sweltering heat. The late-afternoon sun shimmers in a sheen of sweat on her neck.

I step aside to let Rose pass.

"The janitor is on his way to fix the air-conditioning," she says. "Sorry for the inconvenience. Today, we'll only paint one part of the body. Choose a part that fascinates you. Inspires you. Scares you."

Without much enthusiasm in her face, Joni sprawls out on the chaise. Rose traces different parts of her body with her hands, and although she's not actually touching skin, I wish I was in her position.

"Capture them as realistically as you can," she commands.

I don't want to capture. I want to own.

My eyes follow a drop of sweat as it runs between Joni's breasts toward her stretched belly button, where it vanishes in the small oval pit. I trace it with my tongue and suck it up from the curve into which it has melted—the picture so real in my mind, I can actually taste the salt on my tongue.

And then I see it: A small patch of skin that's paler than the rest. A scar, not much longer than my small finger, right above the hairline of her delta. Before I can contemplate it any longer—did she have an accident? surgery? a baby?—the janitor pokes his head into the room. For a second, his eyes fly over Joni's body, excitement flaring in his stare.

I can't blame him. I'm on the same page.

"Air-conditioning's fixed," he says. "Try again, should work now."

Rose thanks him and fumbles with the thermostat. Soon, cold air is flowing through the room, and a shiver runs through Joni's body before becoming a quiver in my own. Chills contract her breasts and turn them into pear-shaped pearls. That's what they look like—two perfect drops made of ivory.

Her nipples stand out, darkened, two smooth nubs amidst patches of wrinkly skin. They're a bit twisted, as if someone had just tweaked them and then stopped time.

Do her breasts fascinate me? Inspire me? All I know right now is that I could fit them nicely into my cupped hands.

Our eyes meet, and Joni blushes.

I want to talk to her. With her. I want to sit in a café with Audra until they ask us to leave because they're closing. I will tell her how I wish I could capture her eyes on paper or in words the way she can portray mine. I will tell her how lonely I feel in my apartment ever since I broke up with Beth. And how I realized that actually, it's not so different from when she was still there. How I'm not missing Beth around, but something else. Something I couldn't really name before I first laid eyes on her in Rose's class.

I will tell her how I love her work lying on my nightstand. How it makes me fall asleep with a little smile on my face every night. Maybe I'll even tell her how I can never have children. And maybe she will wrap her arms around me when I do, and for the first time, it won't feel that devastating.

Joni looks thoughtful, almost sad. There's not a trace of that flirtatious look I thought I caught last week. Maybe this is all in my head. Maybe she never reacted to my drawing. I curse myself for following an impulse. The memory of my rambling about the universe makes me cringe. She probably grinned because I was acting like a prize idiot. But was I wrong to assume she saw behind my façade? Am I a fool for hoping she might have liked what she found?

When the break starts, I scuffle out of the room. The afternoon has tired me in ways I can't quite fathom. As I head down the corridor, I hear quick steps behind me. I turn, and there she is in her kimono, reaching out to me.

"Hi," she says, touching my arm. "Would you like to have coffee?"

LUCKY CHARM

Kate Dominic

Only someone as butch as my Maribelle would love ice fishing. From my princess perspective, no sane woman would sit on a frozen lake for hours on end, wrapped head to toe in insulated gear, staring into a hole while she waited for an icy-cold fish to bite.

Maribelle and her hard water buddies were crazy enough, and my Maribelle was very good with lures. From shiny silver spinners to wriggling live fish, she knew how to reel in what she wanted, even in January on the thick, snow-covered ice of Lake Minnetonka. I loved watching her firm, athletic hips roll beneath her blue and black snowmobile suit as she strode over the ice roads on the lake. Even through all those layers of insulation, I could still envision the way she looked naked under her clothing, her heated muscles moving effortlessly over her ripped, stocky body. And when she held up a prize-sized fish for a picture, her short brown cap of curls framing her strong, wind-reddened face as she grinned into my camera, my pussy tingled and I fell in love all over again.

It was just so damn cold out on the lake! I was once again perched on my camp chair in our hot pink wooden shack, watching the love of my life ladle slush from her freshly augured hole in the thick, gray-white ice. My nose had finally quit running, but the space heater Maribelle had gotten me for Christmas hadn't warmed the interior of the shack up enough for me to so much as loosen my scarf.

Maribelle was all about outdoor sports. I was learning to like being outdoors with her. Last summer, our first together, I'd loved hanging out at the beach in my splashy floral bikini. But I was finding it hard to be trendy in the layers upon layers of clothes under my insulated jacket, heavy snow pants, and insulated mittens. Instead of the sexy new calfskin boots with the three-inch spiked heels Santa had brought me, I was wearing black pack boots with insulated liners over my thick wool hiking socks. Even though my thermals were silk and my sweater merino wool, the only things that really felt right were my bright yellow cashmere face scarf and my designer sunglasses. Don't get me wrong, it's not that I really mind cold all that much. I'm a Minnesota girl through and through. But there's a big difference between dashing from a warm car into an even warmer club or snuggling in front of a fireplace with the woman of my dreams—and sitting on a camp chair inside a tiny, battered wooden ice house.

Maribelle had painted the shack pink for me, much to her disgust. Pink was way too girly for her, but she'd humored me when I pouted. I'd tossed my hair and told her *something* out there on the ice needed to be girly. She'd grabbed me right there in the middle of her backyard and kissed me until my eyes crossed, then she'd pulled the front of my sundress open with her paint-covered finger, peeked down the front, and said she was damn sure there was going to be something girly in her ice house. The back of my dress still sported her handprint from where she'd smacked me as she went back to work.

It was two weeks after Christmas, and Maribelle and her buddies were doing a private, dry-run competition, honing their skills for the big Brainerd ice fishing contest with its $150,000 in prizes. Maribelle had her sights set on the four-wheel drive pickup truck grand prize. Her battered blue Nissan was showing signs of wear and tear from all the backcountry running around we did, every damn month of the year. She was feeling inspired.

I was determined to be her lucky charm, just like the ones in slinky short dresses the gamblers in Vegas had hanging on their arms when they competed for big stakes. I was still getting the feel for how to set the stage in our 10' x 10' ice house. From what I'd seen of the other structures in the shantytown on the lake, most were populated with beer-swilling guys who kept to themselves and spent the day staring at their fish-finding underwater cameras or TVs perched on upturned five-gallon buckets. Our little enclave at the end of the row was all women, but Lydia, Carol, and Nakisha stuck to the bare essentials, too, and everybody on the lake smelled of fish.

Maribelle had told me I could bring whatever I wanted to the shack to entertain myself, so long as all my junk fit in the car and I was willing to schlep it back and forth by myself. And it couldn't be loud or bright enough to scare the fish. At first I'd been bored, bored, *bored*! It was too cold for my brand-new e-book reader, and I couldn't text with my mittens on. The first couple days we'd come to the shack, I'd sulked so much Maribelle had paddled me when we got home.

As usual, that had led to screaming-hot sex. But when she threatened to leave me home if I didn't settle down, I'd changed my approach and started fixing up the shack into my own private ice castle. I'd added a folding table with a lacy tablecloth, camp dishes and a couple of pans, and a stove to cook the stupid little pan fish Maribelle caught. Today's provisions box included cloth napkins, zippered bags of spices and breading, real butter, canned peaches, a single-shot bottle of rum, a bar of Godiva chocolate, and thermoses of hot soup, coffee for Maribelle, and cocoa with marshmallows for me. When I took off the lid to the box, Maribelle rolled her eyes, muttered something about "too femme for words!" and went back to checking her jig line. But when I handed her a mug of coffee, her grin warmed me in all the right places.

Still, it didn't take me long to set up my little nest. This time, I'd brought a real book. And since I have to pee all the time in the cold, especially when I'm drinking cocoa, I'd even bought a little chemical toilet—and I'd gotten silk thermal long johns with old-fashioned drop-flap backs for both Maribelle and me. I'd checked the little weather radio Maribelle had set up on an overturned bucket, making sure no unexpected storms were moving in. None were. With my book in my hand, I settled in to watch Maribelle fish.

Her auger and jig pole rested along the wall beside her. Maribelle was sitting on another bucket, tying a shiny new silver lure onto a line. The lure was part of her plan to perfect a new bouncing technique to entice bigger pan fish to take her bait. My fashionista was wearing her snowmobile suit, black pack boots, and her hunter orange hat with the furry earflaps. Her black insulated gloves and a tackle box were on the snow beside her as she tied a series of tiny knots in the line.

"Are your fingernail clippers handy?"

"Yes, ma'am." I took off my mitten and dutifully handed her the dedicated pair I had tucked in my pocket. My short pink nails were always perfectly manicured, but there was no way I was putting a fishing tool in my makeup bag!

Maribelle clipped the line and handed the clippers back

without looking up. I wrinkled my nose and put them in my pocket. The hut was starting to warm up, so I took my other mitten off and set them on the bucket by the radio. Despite my ridiculous attire, I couldn't help thinking about sex. My bottom tingled pleasantly from last night's spanking, and, well, Maribelle was right there in front of me. Looking at her always turned me on. I poured myself some hot chocolate with marshmallows, and when Maribelle dropped the line in the water, I handed her a cup of steaming hot coffee.

"Thanks." She smiled. Oh, wow—that smile! As always, it sparkled all the way to her eyes. Heated tingles rushed to my pussy and I felt my face heat. God, I loved her!

A moment later, the line jerked. Maribelle set her mug down fast, coffee sloshing onto the snow as she landed a small but legal pan fish onto the ice. The hook was caught hard in its mouth. The fish flopped wildly toward the hole as she tried to dislodge the hook.

"Ew!"

"Quit being such a baby. Where the hell are the needle-nose pliers?"

I'd used them to fix part of the table. I retrieved them and daintily held them out to her. She expertly removed the hook and got up to set the now-nearly-motionless fish in a small bank of snow she'd built up by the door.

"God, you are such a wuss." Her face was red from the still-nippy air and her eyes glowed with pleasure. "First catch," she called out, loud enough for her buddies to hear. Muffled "damns!" echoed from the other shacks.

"But I'm your wuss." I smiled, running my finger seductively up the front of my parka.

She laughed and shook her head at me. "Don't take my tools, baby, unless you put them back. I need them."

"Yes, ma'am." I kept my gaze on her crotch, where she'd more than once strapped on a much-appreciated tool. "I'll take good care of your tools."

She rolled her eyes and sat back down on her bucket. The shack was finally getting warm. She unzipped the top of her snowmobile suit and shrugged out of it, letting it rest around her hips. The thick cable-knit sweater clung to her small, firm breasts. God, I loved playing with Maribelle's breasts. Her nipples were so sensitive. When I rolled the pointy tips between my fingers, her pussy creamed until her juices ran down the side of my hand, especially when I nibbled the side of her neck.

None of those areas were accessible to me at the moment, though my fingers itched to touch them. I pouted into my mug of hot cocoa, my bottom surprisingly tender as I fidgeted against the uncomfortably firm camp chair. Last night, Maribelle had turned me over her knee and smacked me with the hairbrush when I sassed her back once too often about what my attire was going to be on the lake this weekend. That was the first time she'd used the brush, and damn, it turned me on! The flames in my backside fanned the heat building in my pussy. I loved watching Maribelle's breasts move as she jiggled the pole, the way her arms flexed and her hips twisted on her bucket as she lifted another stupid fish from the hole and tossed it to the pile near the door.

"God, you're gorgeous!"

"And you're distracting me." She laughed, calling out "Got another one" to a chorus of muffled curses.

Maribelle had told me to remove layers when I got hot. So even though it was definitely still cool inside the shack, I peeled off my parka and sweater, shivering as I tossed the sweater on the table and quickly pulled my parka back on. My nipples stood up stiff against the thermal shirt. Beneath it, I'd worn only a form-fitting silk camisole. I circled my palms over my nipples, trembling as they tightened to stiff, shadowed points.

"I'm getting really turned on. I bet I could strip down to my boots in here, and nobody but us would notice."

"I'd notice," she growled. "And you'd freeze when I turned you over my knee and unbuttoned the back of those fancy silk drawers. Your pretty little bottom would heat right back up when I commenced to paddle it. But I don't want to scare the fish, and if I have to stop fishing to paddle you, you're going to squeal."

I knew my Maribelle, and I wasn't the only one who got wet when we talked about spanking. Her snowmobile suit unzipped from neck to crotch, and it could be opened from either end. I checked the weather report. Nothing had changed: clear and sunny and, of course, cold.

I moved my chair in back of her and sat down, my thighs spread against her hips as I settled my head comfortably on her shoulder. I carefully rested my hand on her thigh, making sure I didn't bump her arms. They moved up and down as she jiggled the rod. So did her breasts. Her nipples were as stiff as mine. I pretended not to notice.

"I have hat hair." I sighed.

Maribelle's snort vibrated against me. "You have very pretty hat hair. It looks like a lovely, brown mouse nest."

My shriek had Maribelle chuckling even harder. Footsteps crunched on the snow outside the shack.

"What the hell are you two doing in there?" It was Maribelle's friend, Lydia.

"Nothing," I wailed as Maribelle hooted. "Fishing!"

Lydia's snapped "You're scaring the fish" had Maribelle quietly laughing like a loon, and I was pouting all over again, though I couldn't quite make myself move away from the firm, strong body in front of me. Maribelle's breasts were so warm against my hands, and god, my pussy was hot!

"It's important to have attractive hair," I sniffed. Maribelle turned her head, smiling as she kissed me.

"You always have beautiful hair, baby. It's just a little messy from your hood." She reached around and patted the side of my bottom, hard enough to get my attention, though I couldn't really feel it through my snow pants. "Now shush. The under-water camera showed there are fish here. I need to work on my speed."

She picked up the ladle and scooped ice out of the hole, then with a plunk dropped the line into the water again. The silvery shimmer of the lure disappeared into the water. She'd barely begun to jiggle the rod when the line tightened.

"Got another one!" She grinned, pulling up a middle-sized pan fish. "Crappie for dinner."

I wrinkled my nose, averting my eyes as she removed the hook. When she'd cleaned them, I'd cook them. But until they were fillets, they were all Maribelle's. Moments later, the line was back in the water. In the next ten minutes, my love had two more keeper-sized fish lined up on the snow.

Maribelle's face glowed with excitement and her neck was damp with sweat. She worked the line, alternately jiggling it and letting it rest in patterns that made no sense to me. I loved seeing that happy look on her face. I quietly let my hand slide over Maribelle's thigh and into her crotch.

Maribelle turned and gave me a look that promised a very hot bottom later. I smiled innocently and looked studiously at the window. Pretty soon her attention was focused on her line again. As she played with her fishing rod, I carefully slid the bottom of the zipper up. I got it almost to her waist before she noticed.

"Somebody's itching for a spanking."

She had that right. But Maribelle's pants were finally open. I stroked my fingers lightly over the waistband of her thermals, under the edge of her plain white cotton underpants.

"I'm going to turn you over my knee." She was trying to sound gruff, but her voice had that husky sound it got when she was getting really turned on.

"You will," I murmured, "but not now. You're fishing." I gave her my prettiest smile and slid my hand down inside her underpants. Her skin was warm against my fingers. "I'm fishing, too."

I teased my fingers between her pussy lips. Her panties were damp, her slit hot and drenched. I slid my fingers up, and up. Just as I touched her clit, she jumped and her arms jerked.

"Dammit," she panted, her arms straining as she pulled in another fish. "Dammit, I'm fishing!"

"So, fish," I purred. I kept my finger perfectly still as she fought with the fish flopping on the ice. Her thighs tightened around my hand, but she didn't try to push me away. "Pretend we're in Vegas. I'm your lucky charm."

"It's warm in Vegas," she muttered, pulling the fish free and tossing it with the others.

A shadow moved outside the house. Lydia's voice called, "You having any luck?"

"Oh, yeah." Maribelle froze against me. She looked from the window to her crotch and shot me a grin. When she spoke, her voice was cool. "You?"

"I've got a couple. Caro and Nakisha have one each. Nothing much is biting. How about we give it fifteen more minutes, then call it a day. I've got a hot date tonight."

I circled my fingers, then slid them down and into her. Maribelle shuddered against me.

"Fifteen minutes ought to do it," Maribelle choked out.

"Fifteen minutes is good," I whispered, nuzzling her scarf aside so I could bite her neck. I stroked between her now-drenched pussy lips, alternately nipping and sucking her neck. I slipped my other hand up under her arm, lifting her sweater and thermal, pulling down the front of her bra. Her nipple stiffened in the cold. I pinched, warming the straining tip with the friction of my fingers, tugging it out into the chilly winter air.

"I going to paddle you with the hairbrush," she choked. "I'm going to paddle until you yell."

"Mm-hmm." I sucked the side of her neck hard. "I bet you'll really heat my bottom."

"Like it's been too close to the fire," she panted, arching into my fingers. "Oh, baby, that feels so good!"

I slid three fingers deep, rubbing my thumb relentlessly over her clit. "I love it when you spank me, especially when you paddle me with your grandma's antique maple hairbrush. It sets my pussy on fire."

Maribelle thrust rhythmically against my hand, letting me fuck her with my fingers as I milked her nipple. She turned her head to me, plunging her tongue into my mouth. Her pussy juice was running down the side of my hand. I curled my fingers inside her, ruthlessly rubbing her clit as I pressed up hard. I caught her scream into my mouth as she shuddered against me.

Suddenly, her arms jerked hard. Her velvety warm pussy walls clamped down around my fingers. She swore and leaned harder into me, ignoring the straining rod as she trembled and groaned.

"I am paddling your ass good for this," she gasped. "And you are so replacing my lure!"

The rod had stopped jerking, the line obviously snapped. Swearing, Maribelle pulled away and put the rod under her foot.

"Stand up and pull those fancy snow pants down to your ankles. Then unbutton your drawers and bend over."

"Yes, ma'am!" My fingers flew over the ridiculous amount of clothes I was wearing, then I was bending over in front of her, my boots planted wide, my hands on my knees, my thermals unbuttoned, and my pussy backed up even with my Maribelle's wicked lashing tongue. She snapped my thong with one yank, then grabbed my hips and buried her face in my slit. She tongued me until I was ready to scream. Then she sucked my clit until I wailed my orgasm into the fist I had stuffed in my face.

I was trembling so hard I had to sit down. I had barely stepped away when Maribelle's "Dammit!" echoed through the shack. The rod had jerked out from under her foot, catching on the edge of the hole. She grabbed it up, her arms bulging as she fought the rod that was now bent so far over I was certain it was going to break. I jerked my pants up right over my unbuttoned thermals, staring in shock as Maribelle fought to bring in her fish.

"Is everybody all right in here?" The door flew open as Lydia and Caro and Nakisha ran in. We all stared in shock as a huge, ugly walleye head broke through the icy film that had been forming over the hole. As the three of them yelled encouragement, handing her gaffs and hooks and god knows what else, Maribelle dragged a fifteen-inch walleye through the hole. If anybody noticed the condition of my Maribelle's pants, they politely didn't mention it. They were all too busy hooting and hollering and taking pictures and wondering why the line hadn't snapped and expounding on theories about what kind of bait she'd used. The general consensus was that the original crappie she'd caught hadn't broken the line, it had just become bait for the walleye, though nobody but me could quite figure out why she'd left the crappie in the water for so long.

Maribelle still paddled my butt with the hairbrush when we got home. She got my bottom so hot and tingly and sore, and she made me come so hard I howled like a wolf crying to the winter moon. And afterward, my Maribelle told me that I could be her lucky charm and come as often as I liked every time we went ice fishing in our hot pink ice house, though I'd have to keep my clothes on at the actual competitions, since those were held out in the open.

I couldn't wait to go shopping for my new ice-fishing wardrobe. We had weeks more of hard ice. I was so going to make the most of it.

THE COLOR OF AUTUMN

Joey Bass

"Look me in the eye and say that to my face." I stared into brown eyes, pupils almost indiscernible, and growled. "You don't know who I am. You don't know what I can do. Believe me, you don't wanna see me angry." There was a knock at the door, but I didn't care. I pointed at the face before me. "*You* have the power. They don't know what you can do. They're fools. Remember that. Feel the power, your power." The knock came again, this time louder, but I would not be distracted. I didn't look away as I placed my leather-clad palm on the mirror and took a deep breath, exhaling through my nose. "One with the All," I said with conviction, letting out another low growl. I flexed my hand and made a fist, feeling the leather of my finger-less gloves hug my knuckles. "You have the power, the will, the desire. They have noth—" The doorknob rattled and shook, stopping my words with the fear that the warped door wasn't securely shut. I quickly removed my gloves and shoved them inside my leather jacket.

"Dizzy, what the hell are you doing in there? I gotta dry my hair." Megan's voice hissed through the door. Our baby brother was still asleep and we knew better than to wake him. Ever since Jake was born, we had perfected our hissing techniques.

Running my fingers through my damp dark curls, I turned away from my reflection and silently surrendered the bathroom to my older sister.

"Jeez, Dizz. The time you spend in there, you'd think you actually were trying to look good, but you come out in those same old jeans and your hair all wet." Megan brushed past me. Her fluffy pink robe smelled of watermelons and some sweeter body wash.

I couldn't imagine smelling like a fruit basket. I wondered why some girls preferred fruit over flowers. Ryan Harlen started smelling faintly of roses right after Easter when we were in sixth grade. Monica Rivas, on the other hand, sometimes smelled of fresh bread because she helped her mother make tortillas some mornings. Both of them smelled nice and the odors were light and clean, not clinging like my sister's syrupy smell.

"You're lucky people don't start calling you Fonzie. Of course, he *combed* his hair, but still…" Megan pulled a hair-dryer from under the sink while continuing with her teasing, even though I was almost out of earshot. "That's such an old show, no one but archeologists would know what it was. So count yourself lucky, Dizzy. I watched an episode on the Internet. It was pretty funny, but you are totally Fonzie, without all the cool moves or the popularity."

I loved Megan, but sometimes I didn't feel lucky to have such a popular older sister. Megan was a cheerleader and senior class president. She had always been popular, and I imagined she always would be. No matter where she would go in her life, Megan would win every contest: Miss Pig-tails at the Pork

Festival, Miss Artichoke, Miss Sugar Beet, Miss Mars Colony. Megan was even voted prom queen at the junior-senior prom when she was only a freshman. I would more likely get hit by lightning than get asked to a dance, not that I even really thought about going. I found most of the people at my school to be rather dull, except for a few of the teachers.

Megan's blow dryer hummed away in the bathroom as I slipped on my backpack and headed downstairs. I grabbed a grapefruit and a can of Coke from the fridge. School was about a mile from the house, and I didn't mind walking. I had time to walk and peel my breakfast.

"Desiree, don't forget you have to watch Jake tonight, so no goofing around after school." My mother's muffled voice floated up the laundry chute from the basement. "Come right home."

Pausing with my hand on the doorknob, I stared at the offending cabinet beside me. Why did my mom always think that I goofed off after school? I was working, mucking out stables and mowing lawns. I got paid for those jobs. Babysitting little Jake while my mother went to a Pilates class never gave me more than a headache.

I opened the cabinet to peer down the chute. I could see my mother's arm and hand reaching, sorting through the pile of dirty laundry. "Sure, Mom. I won't forget, but when you get home I have two jobs to do. So I'd appreciate that you didn't hang out with all your pill-latte buddies." I didn't try to keep the annoyance from my voice.

"Desi, I can't be sure how late I'll be. Just call them and tell them you'll take care of it tomorrow." My mother sounded tired.

I sighed. We'd gone over this a lot. She knew that I had more jobs to do the next day, so I couldn't easily switch them to other days. I would end up working straight through the weekend.

Not that it mattered, not much else to do. But it was a matter of principle. Teenagers should be able to loaf around on the weekends. Plus I wanted to get through another dungeon level of *Bodacious Blades*. "Can you ask Megan to take over at four-thirty if you aren't home? She won't listen to me."

"Not happening!" Megan's voice erupted from above. The chute opened into the bathroom as well. "I can't. I have a study date."

"Girls, please, just work it out, okay? I have a deadline coming up and I need your help. Desi, you watch Jake until five and then Megan, you take over."

Megan protested while I heartily agreed and made a hasty exit. If Megan actually showed up, I'd have at least two hours of daylight left to get both jobs done.

I'd just finished peeling my grapefruit and tossed the last bit of skin into the ivy that bordered the Johnsons' old place when a soft voice called out to me. *"Bonjour, belle-fille."*

Naturally, I froze, wedge of fruit halfway to my mouth. I couldn't figure out where the voice had come from. I didn't see anyone nearby.

"Ai je vous…oh sorry, did I startle you?" The voice floated down from the heavens. Soft and lilting, and very French sounding.

I looked up and found that there was indeed a girl above me, but she was not floating. Rather, she was in a tree. And although her voice was heavenly, she had no wings and looked to be flesh—not an angel. The sun danced on what could only be described as a waterfall of light copper hair. "You're in the Johnsons' elm tree," I said. Smooth as always—stating the obvious. *Dork.*

The girl smiled, a dazzling row of white teeth appeared and disappeared as she said, "I am in a tree. I have no doubt."

I nodded, proving my total lack of functioning synapses.

"Do you go to Pleasant Valley?" the girl asked, dangling a red Converse at me.

"Yeah." I nodded again, finally spitting out a single syllable. *Brilliant.*

"I'm glad you came by. I could really use your help today. We can go together. Two can fit on my scooter." With each sentence she spoke, the girl moved closer to the ground, weaving among the branches. Her movement was relaxed and fluid.

My heart pounded as I watched her maneuver from limb to limb. Shimmering copper hair swayed around her as it spilled over her shoulders and fought with the hood of her sweatshirt. When she reached the ground, the girl stuck out her hand and said, "Angela Hart, very nice to meet you."

Angel...Heart? Manga comic book title? I looked at the wedge of grapefruit I held, unable to shake the hand that was extended. My other hand held the rest of the grapefruit and dangled like a broken chicken wing, unable to move because of the can of soda I had in the crook of my arm. "Uh, Bowman."

"Is that your name or a job title?" She plucked the fruit wedge from my fingers.

"Huh?" *Such a wordsmith.*

She seemed pleased. "Well, Bowman," she said and took a bite of the wedge. Juice squirted out and dripped down her fingers to her palm. "You have just met that tree's new *compadre*, and she adores swinging and eating grapefruit."

My brain registered the words but my mouth didn't know how to respond. My mind was still processing what they meant. Did this mean that I had a new neighbor? *An amazingly awesome neighbor*, which struck me as odd because I had never met anyone remotely interesting and this girl captivated me, literally froze me to that spot on the sidewalk.

A horn blared behind me. I recognized the deep rumbling of Megan's boyfriend's Cougar. I heard our front door slam.

"Dizzy! You still here? You're gonna be late." Megan's voice rose above the growling engine. The car door squeaked open and slammed shut as the engine revved and gears shifted. I began to turn around when Angela took the rest of the grapefruit from me and tore it in half, recapturing my attention. More juice dripped over her hands. I was mesmerized by those hands. The Cougar rolled to a stop at the curb. "Come on, Dizz. Get in. You're going to be late."

Megan was talking to me, but I couldn't look away from those fingers as they moved the wedge of glistening fruit toward two smiling lips. *Puffy lips. Angela's lips. They look so soft.*

Angela let out a soft giggle, handing one half of the grapefruit back. "Dizz." She chuckled quietly.

"What are you, high?" Megan shouted as her boyfriend revved the engine. "Stop spacing and get in. We can give your little friend a ride too, if she needs it."

My little friend. I fought to get my thoughts in order as I nodded, then shook my head. My gaze met Angela's and my mind rattled on. *Amber...topaz...Angel Heart...*

Angela saved me from having to respond. She waved the Cougar away saying, "Don't worry about it. Thanks anyway. She's coming with me."

Megan's response was lost in the squeal of rubber on asphalt as Christopher pulled away from the curb. The screeching tires managed to pull my gaze away from Angela's shimmering gold-brown eyes. I watched the midnight blue Cougar speed toward the school, exhaust cloud spewing from the chrome tailpipe.

"Tiger's-eye," I announced matter-of-factly.

"Pardon?" Angela's gaze swept down my body, and she stared for a moment at my knee.

I looked down at my leg, wondering what had caught Angela's attention. Nothing seemed amiss. *Fly's not down.* "Um, your eyes are gold and brown…with a depth to the colors." My heart did a light jig. "You know, like a…like a tiger's-eye rock."

"Sweet. I always knew I had rocks in my head." Without warning she bent at the hips and vigorously patted down my shin and calf.

"What the—" I was too surprised to move away.

"Thought you had a gun in your boot." She turned on her heels. "Come on. We don't want to be late on my first day of school."

I didn't move at first. I had just realized that Angela no longer had any hint of a French accent, and for a moment I wondered if I was still in bed dreaming.

"Follow me if you want to ride." Angela lifted her arm like a tour guide without even turning around.

This girl…this girl…is…something. But my conclusions were lost as I watched the swaying hips quickly move away. Angela wore navy sweatpants and a gray hoodie. Nothing remotely sexy, but for some reason that word popped right into my mind. Once again, I was shocked by these new thoughts. I didn't move as I focused on my boots. Then I noticed dark smudges on my pant leg. At first I wondered how it'd gotten wet, but then the image flashed in my mind. *Gun in my boot, huh? She wiped her sticky hands on my leg! That little—*

Herhonk! Herhonk!

The sound of an old-fashioned bike horn yanked me out of my head. I looked up to find Angela, wearing an old leather aviator's cap and goggles, sitting on a rusty tandem bicycle with a coffee can attached below the handlebars. Copper hair disappeared into her collar. "Come on, Bowman. Let's go."

As my feet propelled me forward, my mind began to realize

that the coffee can was part of the bike and there appeared to be some type of motor resting below it on the bike frame. *Hell no. It's some kind of Frankenstein moped!* The image of Angela welding together old bikes in the middle of the night suddenly came to mind. The goggles she was now wearing probably protected her eyes during her experiments.

"Come on, we only have to pedal a little and I can pop-start it."

I tested the old leather seat to see if it was loose, pushing and pulling it firmly.

"Don't worry. It's a Darny," she explained, as if that would make everything clear.

I slipped my still unopened soda into my jacket and tightened my backpack straps. After swinging my leg over the bike seat, I straddled the bar and rested one foot on a pedal but didn't sit down. I had never ridden tandem or on the back of anyone's scooter. My head was surprised at what my body was doing, and my heart was auditioning for *Riverdance*, but my voice felt strong and steady. "You give the count of three and we push off, right?"

"No, just get on the seat and get ready to pedal. I'm holding it."

I was worried about my own ability to balance, but I didn't want Angela to think I was scared, so I hoisted myself onto the seat. It was an ancient thing and felt like cold, hard steel. I was relieved that the seat and handlebars seemed secure, but I wasn't going to test fate by pulling up on the bars. "Okay. I'm ready."

Angela leaned forward and shouted as if the motor was already engaged, "Good. Get ready to pedal. Here we go!"

As soon as Angela's foot left the ground, I pedaled and propelled us forward. I was surprised by how easy Angela made it seem. I had expected an old rusty crank—chains slipping and grinding—but the pedals moved smoothly. Without warning a chuckle escaped from my chest and rolled out of my mouth.

"What are you laughing at, Bowman? Surprised that my pile of tin hasn't fallen apart?"

"Naw, it's just…I dunno…maybe." I felt myself smiling.

"Ah, Bo, you ain't seen nothin' yet. This is a good speed. Keep pedaling, okay, no matter what happens."

"Huh, whaddya mean? No matter—" Angela's laughter stopped my words.

"Bo, relax. I'm not gonna let anything happen to you okay? Just pedal."

I obeyed as a buzz saw cranked to life and the bike lurched forward. My grip on the handlebars tightened. I was startled by the speed, but managed to be amused. "Whoa. We're riding a weed whacker!"

"Vámonos! Nous allons."

The old moped whirred like an angry hornets' nest, but it held together. My wrists and butt bones felt every crack and penny on the pavement, but the seat and handlebars stayed intact. As we neared the school, traffic increased, but it wasn't until we were in the parking lot that I began to worry about what we looked like. People were staring, some even turning around and pointing.

"Hey, Yes-sir-ree, you visit the freak aisle and buy yourself a friend?" someone yelled as Angela cut the engine. The nickname was from second grade when a substitute teacher mispronounced my name.

I leaned forward to tell Angela where to park. Beyond the smell of the old leather cap was a comforting smell, a pleasant scent that wasn't entirely new to me. It reminded me of Christmas. It was a subtle smell of pine and something else I couldn't quite name. Cinnamon, a hint of nutmeg, and maybe roasted chestnuts with the promise of a warm wood-burning fireplace.

"Blue light special on the freak aisle, more like it," Sheila Saunders yelled.

I recognized her voice. I had grown up with Sheila. *Kinky blond whore.*

"Rusty aisle on the freak light," Paul Philips chimed in as he rolled by on his skateboard. "Hangers and paper clips!"

"Dammit, Paulie, you lit or just stupid?"

"Both, dude." Paul's laughter was swallowed by the din of the other students milling about.

I was hoping the bell would ring soon because that meant people would be more focused on getting into the school than harassing us. We slowed to a stop, each putting a foot down and dismounting. It was as if we had done it before. *Beginner's luck*, I reasoned.

Angela removed her goggles and cap. She grinned from ear to ear. "Wasn't that great?"

I nodded, surprised that Angela didn't seem affected by the overt stares and taunting that had greeted us. "Seat stayed on and so did my ass."

"Successful first run. Now, where's the principal's office?"

"First run?" I gasped. The thing could have exploded or imploded...whatever Frankenstein-mobiles did.

With a stern look of determination, she marched forward, linked her arm through mine, and began pulling me by the elbow. "I wanna get there before the bell rings."

I had never walked arm in arm with anyone and found it rather awkward. I bounced when Angela dipped. She bobbed when I weaved. We were so out of sync that I wasn't surprised when she released me.

Bumping me with her hip, she exclaimed, "Walk much? Relax, Bowman. You're not gettin' graded here. Not a catwalk."

I tried to smile. Tried to relax. But we were getting judged.

I could feel the other students looking at me, judging, and condemning me for being different. Abnormal. Odd. Queer. The bell rang as a shiver ran up my spine and tickled the back of my head. *A freak…*

"Dammitshitloretta," Angela hissed, grabbing my arm again and tugging me forward as we entered the school. "We're late. Stop goofing around."

"I'm not goofing," I protested as Angela picked up speed. "No running in the halls, Miss Hart," I teased, allowing her to pull me into a slow jog.

When we reached the two double doors marked *Gym*, Angela stopped and spun toward me. "Where's the damn office?"

I pointed a thumb over my shoulder. "Back this way and to the left."

"Bowman, why didn't you say something?"

"I was too busy being pulled after you." In truth I was too busy watching her hair, the color of autumn, as it swayed with her movement.

"Ladies, where are you supposed to be?" a stern voice broke in between us.

"Ms. Riggins." I nodded. "Good morning, ma'am."

"*Bonjour, Madam Riggins.*" Angela's French accent was back in full swing.

"Oh, are you the new student?" Ms. Riggins's voice filled with sugar.

"*Oui*, very nice to meet you. My name is Angela Hart."

"Well, Miss Hart, you should report to the principal's office straight away."

"*Oui oui. Je suis désolée, Madam*, I asked Mademoiselle Desiree to show me the school. I did not know it was so late. How shameful of me."

"Desiree should have known better."

Angela reeled me to her side. Our elbows and shoulders knocked together. "*Oui oui*, Desiree tried to tell me. I am sure. But I was so...so persimmon. It could not be helped."

As I watched their exchange, my jaw lost the will to hold my chin up. I could feel my mouth opening and was unable to close it. But when Angela said "persimmon" I had to force it shut to keep from laughing.

"I'm sure the principal won't be too upset with you. Just go there now." Ms. Riggins pulled the heavy doors open and strode into the darkness of the gymnasium.

"*Merci beaucoup*," Angela called after her.

A guffaw escaped my lips.

Angela turned to me and raised her eyebrows. "Not very ladylike, that sound."

"Your acc—" A quick peck on the lips stopped my words momentarily. "You just—"

Angela's vise grip on the sleeve of my jacket pinned me to her side as she spun away from the gym and cut off my words again.

"Your face is red," she said matter-of-factly.

"What the—" Another kiss, this time on my cheek. "Fuck," I managed to say.

"No time. Gotta see the principal." Angela suddenly released me and strode away.

Once again I found myself unable to move as I watched those swaying hips. Those hips, that hair, her voice, those lips.

She raised her hand. "Come with me if you don't want to get written up."

And once again, I followed Angela Hart, not really knowing what to do or think. I was just putting one foot in front of the other, following that shimmering hair, that amazing copper-gold hair, following those swaying hips. What else could I do? Go to my first-period class and watch numbers dancing on the blackboard? Not a chance! The other students in the hallway faded to mere shadows. I no longer cared who they were or what they were thinking. I was who I was and Angela Hart wanted me to follow her. A feeling of great happiness and well-being filled me. It was right.

I didn't fully realize it or know what it meant, but a part of me knew. My heart? My brain? My soul. A part of me knew I would follow those swaying hips and that waterfall hair anywhere, and I would be doing it for years.

V-DAY DIARIES

Mette Bach

Out for dinner with Lara, my ex-who-is-now-my-friend, we enjoyed the same souvlaki we always have. We still go to "our place," and the closeness is still there. But, unlike me, Lara is a hopeless romantic. She left me for another hopeless romantic years ago but, as often happens between hopeless romantics, they both fell hard and Lara moved from the West Coast to the East Coast to be with her new perfect girlfriend. At first, I was bitter. I was sad to see her go, annoyed by her gloating, and more determined than ever to think of romance as a bunch of hogwash. For at least a year afterward, it felt to me that all romance was good for was putting money in the pockets of card company executives. It would have been really easy to turn my back on Lara when her perfect romance ended horribly but, ironically, I didn't have the heart. Against my own desire, I had missed her. When she called me, her voice muffled and choked up over her breakup, I couldn't help but console her. I was glad she was moving back to the West Coast, even though she did so reluctantly, heartbroken.

Since she has moved back, things have been very different between us. She is single. I have a girlfriend. I try not to rub it in her face. I learned not to treat people the way I don't like to be treated, so whenever we get together I try to minimize my new relationship, just so she doesn't use my happiness as an excuse to beat herself up.

"How's Betty?" she asked.

"Oh fine. Good. She's good."

"So you two are serious, huh?"

"Yeah." I thought back to the way she used the word *serious* when we were together, how she pushed for more of it and how it annoyed me.

"So you think you'll be moving in together?"

"Hell no," I said. "You know me. I like living alone. Remember?"

"How could I forget?"

My not wanting to move in together was a source of much frustration for her. I sipped my iced tea and felt gratitude for Betty, who, like me, is independent and does not want to live together.

The conversation turned to Valentine's Day, that pain-in-the-arse holiday mere weeks away.

"What are you doing for Betty?" Lara wanted to know.

"I'm not sure."

"You don't have anything planned?"

"You know how I feel about V-Day. I prefer February fifteenth, the biggest chocolate sale of the season."

"You're incorrigible," she said.

"I found someone to spend time with on Valentine's Day," my friend Cass told me one night at Denny's. "She's also single, so it's perfect."

"That's great." I slurped on my Orange Crush float and dipped my French fry into the diminishing dollop of ketchup on my plate.

"What are you doing on V-Day?" she asked.

"I dunno," I said.

"Well, aren't you doing something with Betty?"

"Maybe. We haven't really talked about it," I confessed, feeling as I was speaking the words that my tone was too nonchalant for her liking.

"But it's next week already."

"Yeah."

"And places fill up. I mean, if you want reservations or whatnot, you have to act fast." She plunged her fork into a broccoli floret.

"Well, I'm working that night anyway, so dinner is out of the question."

"But you'll see each other afterward, right?" She sounded concerned.

"Maybe. Like I said, we haven't really talked about it."

"Is everything okay? I mean, between the two of you?" She leaned in, like she was ready for me to spill my guts and give me a shoulder to cry on.

Earlier that week a different friend emailed me an essay-length stressed-out cry for help. Her best friend is single this Valentine's Day and she feels bad for her so she is organizing a bouquet of flowers and a box of chocolates to be sent to her friend's workplace. She emailed me because she knows I read poetry and wanted some hints for something really romantic to put in the card.

"Stay away from *The Love Song of J. Alfred Prufrock*," I advised. I told her the truth, which is that the poetry I like has very little business on a Valentine's card. Finally, I thought back all the way to high school and suggested one of Shakespeare's sonnets. She wrote back and said that she couldn't use Shakespeare, that it was just too much and she's signing the card *from a secret admirer* and she doesn't want her friend to completely freak out. I guess Shakespeare is freakout material.

In my next email to her, I suggested that Hallmark was probably her best bet. I also told her I thought her plan was pretty elaborate. She's even getting her brother to pay the florist in cash so that nothing can be traced back to her, just in case her friend tries. It struck me as partly sweet and partly psychotic to trick her friend like that.

She wrote me back and said, "Yeah, well, it's Valentine's Day, and you know how single women are on Valentine's Day."

Valentine's Day only means one thing to me: getting in trouble. It never fails. Whether I'm attached or single, I seem to screw up on Valentine's Day every single year because invariably I make the mistake of confessing that I don't believe in it. The Romans believed that February was the best month to procreate, so in order to facilitate as many pregnancies as possible, many engaged in the Bacchanalian festivals—orgies of booze and sex and sweet times. That is something I can wrap my mind around. That tradition continued well into the Middle Ages. Somewhere along the way, the church needed to sanctify all the sex being had, so, conveniently, a patron saint was ushered in. There are four different saints named St. Valentine. Which one believed in romance and fairy-tale endings? No one really knows. By the 1900s, businesses had figured out that they could make a lot of money on people's idealistic romantic pursuits. Consumerism went from reasonable to perverse within a century, and now, here we are buying teddy bears and cinnamon hearts and lingerie and flowers and chocolate. But I have learned to shut up about it.

I open my big mouth and talk about consumerism and cash grabbing and fairy-tale nonsense and I have come to under-stand—finally, after decades—that nobody wants to hear it.

One year my best friend called me in tears because her boyfriend got her a potted plant.

"What's wrong with that?" I asked, totally clueless.

"What's wrong! You don't get your girlfriend a potted plant on Valentine's Day. You just don't."

I felt sorry for him. I've managed to be the giver of the potted plant style of gift myself. Unintentionally, I've ruined many Valentine's Days for many people.

With my tail tucked ever so slightly between my legs, I broached the topic with my girlfriend.

"So, um, Valentine's Day is coming up," I began.

"Yeah, I've been meaning to ask you if that's something you care about."

"Me? Nope. You?"

"Nope."

"Really?" I wondered if perhaps there really was such a thing as a soul mate.

"Nah. Actually, some of my most memorable Valentine's Days are the ones I've spent by myself," she said.

Words cannot express the love and gratitude that came over me as she told me about the time her roommate walked in on her wooing herself with takeout and wrestling on Super Channel.

"Me too," I said, and told her about the time I took myself out for a large mocha and a brownie with whipped cream and read Angela Carter stories for hours at my favorite coffee shop.

"If you want to do something for V-Day, we could," she said. "Like dinner or whatever."

"Oh, I could give a crap."

The words came straight from my heart. They were honest and sincere and it made me tear up just to be able to speak them without fearing judgment.

"Valentine's Day just strikes me as a really stupid excuse for women to beat themselves up for what they perceive as imperfections in their lives," my girlfriend said.

I hugged her and told her that might very well be the most romantic thing anyone has ever said.

When V-Day arrives, I want to tell her that she's the Prince Charming to my Cinderella or the Cinderella to my Prince Charming, whichever one she wants to be. But I hold back. Neither one of us has any business in glass slippers.

We both go to work, like usual. I watch all the bouquet-carrying people on the bus and wonder where they're off to and why they aren't all beaming with joy. It's ironic to me that this holiday is supposed to be a celebration of love but instead it's some kind of awful test. In spite of Betty's and my conversation, I still can't help but wonder if it is a test I will fail.

But then I receive the answer in the form of a text message: *Thai food? Our place? Eight o'clock?*

I confirm instantly. I stop in at the drugstore to pick up some dish detergent and vitamin C. I pause in the candy aisle, wondering if she is expecting something even if she says she isn't. I resist the temptation to buy chocolate. It's not that I don't want to give her chocolate. I love buying chocolate for her. I love giving her things. I love spending time with her. It's just that the rebel in me doesn't want to do that today. Not on V-Day.

So I show up empty-handed at the Thai restaurant and so does she. We get takeout, walk back to my place and just before we get to my building, we stop and kiss each other on the sidewalk in the rain.

"I love you," I say.

"I love you too," she says.

"This is totally my idea of a perfect V-Day. I hope it's yours too. It's not too late to go out for a nice dinner if you'd rather."

"No way," she says. "If we do that, we have to keep our pants on. I'd rather make this a pant-free evening."

"You're my dream woman," I tell her. "Happy Valentine's Day."

NIGHT AT THE WAX MUSEUM

Delilah Devlin

12:02 A.M.—Remind V.H. to call the exterminators. Rats, again, in the vicinity of the freak show exhibit!

Krista Pike clicked the end of her ballpoint pen, slid the small spiral notebook into her pocket and clipped the pen in her uniform lapel. Then she slipped her Maglite from its holster, picked up a sturdy broom and went in search of the rodent.

For the third night in a row her nerves were wired tighter than an M16's recoil spring. Shouldn't have been. The security company that'd hired her told her that other than some minor vandalism to the museum's windows and door, this shift should be a cakewalk.

"Tell that to the fucking rats."

A skittering sounded behind her. She spun and aimed her light toward the floor. Nothing. As she raised the beam, it caught the exhibit. Light flickered in the eyes of the wax figure lying in the open coffin—a scene straight out of a horror movie, created especially for the Halloween crowd.

She shivered at the tableau. A raven-haired vampire, red glassy eyes, milky-white skin, the tops of her breasts exposed above the black, corseted gown, not a hint of color in her or the white-satin-lined coffin other than blood-red paint on her full lips. Above her, the vampire hunter stood with arms raised, a hammer and a wooden stake in his hands, ready to puncture her chest. The setting surrounding the two figures was straight Hollywood kitsch—a gnarled tree, an open pit readied for the coffin and a tall Celtic cross knocked at an angle.

The overhead track light beamed directly on the vampire's face, and her glass eyes appeared to be fixed right on Krista.

Krista shivered and aimed the beam back to the ground, unsure which creeped her out more now, the rats or the red glowing lights the artist had placed behind the wax figure's eye sockets.

She moved along, scuffing her feet to make enough noise to scare away any critters looking for discarded scraps of popcorn or candy bars that patrons of the wax museum had tossed.

Damn nerves. She needed to make an appointment with her VA shrink to up her meds. Problem solved. Total pisser she still needed those damn happy pills. Until she had a clean bill of health, the PD wouldn't clear her for duty again. And there was no way she wanted to return full-time to the force without being whole again. Eighteen months in Afghanistan had left her in little broken bits. Shattered hip. Shattered mind.

A year of therapy—for the bones and her mushed brain— and she still wasn't 100 percent. Not when a goddamn rat could spook her like this.

She was tempted to hit the utility closet and turn on all the lights just as she had last night, but the manager had chewed her ass for wasting electricity. She was stuck with the thin beams illuminating the exhibits, making the surrounding darkness feel dense and alive.

Another shiver shook her. "Fuck this," she bit out, pissed at herself for letting the place get to her. Maybe she should move on to the presidents. Nothing scary there other than the looming height and craggy face of Honest Abe.

The skittering sounded again, behind her. She spun and crouched, flashlight held like a nightstick, the broom like a sword, blood pumping every bit as hard as when her squad had come under fire in Kandahar. She'd shimmied under a burned-out van only to discover she didn't have enough room between the road and the vehicle's undercarriage to effectively return fire. She'd scooted back the way she'd come, but the battle was already over. Or so she'd thought. Kneeling beside Randy Hays's body, she'd caught a round in her ass, another in her torso, which the Kevlar ate, but the impact had still been strong enough to knock the breath out of her.

"Fuck this," she repeated, her voice sounding every bit as hollow as her resolve. Her beam caught the edge of the coffin, glared on the white lining of the lid. She moved on—then swung her light back to the bed of the casket. It was empty.

Not a goddamn rat. Someone else was inside the museum and playing a nasty trick.

"Not fucking funny," she said, straightening and aiming her voice around the room.

Soft laughter came from right behind her, and Krista punched her elbow backward and whirled, but again saw nothing except for a blur of gray.

Her breath caught. Nothing moved that fast. Straightening, she tossed down the broom.

"I know you're here," she said, deepening her voice, hoping whoever or whatever it was couldn't tell how freaked she was.

"I've been watching you," came a feminine, singsong voice.

Krista jerked, then cursed herself for giving away her fear.

"Come out of the shadows. I'll walk you to the door and let you leave. I won't call it in."

"How sweet." The voice was girlish, almost childlike, but with an undertone of menace that chilled Krista to the bone. "Why do you limp?"

Krista breathed deeply, calming her heart. The voice had come from near the door leading to the Marilyn exhibit. Krista didn't know if the woman had a weapon or was just a thrill seeker. There wasn't anything of value inside the museum other than big wax dolls. Nothing irreplaceable. The cash box was cleaned out every night after closing. "Why'd you move the vampire?"

Another laugh. This one so close the hairs on the back of her neck stirred.

"Pretty boy, I didn't take it."

"I'm not a boy," she said, more to keep the conversation going than because she'd been offended.

"But you act like one. Even walk like one."

"I was a soldier."

"And they made you walk that way?"

"I don't have girly hips."

A hand cupped one notch of her uninjured hip from behind. A citrusy-floral scent tickled her nose. Something wet slid down the side of her neck. A tongue. Panic shivered down her spine.

"Not boy's hips." A hand trailed down the front of her pants, and fingers traced her split. "Not a boy's anything at all."

Krista didn't know why she stayed so still. She wasn't a superstitious person. Didn't believe in ghosts or God. But she knew in her gut whatever was behind her wasn't human. As fast as the thing had moved, she couldn't outrun it. "You're that woman in the coffin, aren't you?"

"Not stupid like a boy either. Not like the last one."

"The last guard?"

"They didn't tell you?"

Krista shook her head. "I wasn't told why he had to be replaced." Fingers walked across the top of her shoulder and up her neck, pads skimming over her thudding pulse. Krista swayed, her eyelids dipped.

"Poor thing couldn't hold his bladder. All I had to do was blow in his ear and he'd shriek—"

"Like a girl?"

The laugh this time sounded more natural. Hands drew away.

She blinked and the raven-haired creature stood in front of her, her gaze studying Krista's face. "You're different."

"Than what? There are other female guards employed by Security Systems."

"Not what I meant. You're not frightened of me."

"Sure I am, but the rats creeped me out more."

"Rats won't kill you."

"I'm not afraid of dying."

The woman stepped closer, tilting her head to gaze up into Krista's eyes. "I can see that. But why?"

Krista felt her throat close up, and cleared it. "Dying's easy."

The woman lifted her lips in a snarl, exposing the twin points of her upper canines. "For some, perhaps." Her head turned toward the windows at the front of the museum. "It's morning."

"It's just after midnight," Krista said, raising her arm to glance at her watch, but it was 6:30 A.M. "What the...?"

When she glanced back up, the woman was gone. Krista darted a glance at the exhibit. The woman was falling back into the coffin, as though in slow motion, her hair and gown billowing, then settling around her.

Krista dipped beneath the velvet ropes surrounding the

exhibit, ignoring the twinge in her hip, and climbed onto the platform. She bent over the woman as she clasped her hands over her stomach. Their gazes locked for a moment, and then life left the vampire's eyes.

She lay still. Silent.

Krista cupped her fingers beneath the woman's nose. No breath. Her chest unmoving. She touched her lips. Hard and cold.

Drawing back, she gazed down. "But you didn't tell me your name."

The next night, Krista arrived at 6:15 P.M.

"You're late," the manager said, frowning.

"Sorry about that. Got caught in traffic." A lie, but she didn't want to admit she'd fought a battle with herself that she'd lost. When she'd rolled out of bed, her hand had gone to the phone, ready to quit. She'd even punched the numbers to the office, but she'd hesitated.

She'd convinced herself she'd imagined the whole thing. A drug-induced dream. Then she'd dumped her meds into the toilet. Last night couldn't be real.

Still, once the door closed behind her, she headed straight to the horror exhibits. Everything was just as it had been. The woman stretched out in the coffin, unmoving, looking as waxy pale as any other life-sized wax figure.

However, this wax doll was different. Every detail perfect from the fine, feminine down on her cheeks and sparse nose hairs to the girly parts no visitor to the museum would ever see.

She cupped the front of the vampire hunter's crotch and found it smooth. The artist hadn't bothered to create genitalia where it would be hidden beneath clothing. When she played with the vampire's silk bodice, plucking it to peer beneath the fabric, she found perfectly rendered nipples—painted a lovely, rosy pink. Feeling like a perv, she backed off the platform before she gave in to the urge to check beneath the figure's skirt.

Hours rolled by and nothing happened. Disappointment weighed down her shoulders. Part of her had wanted last night's experience to be real. Not just because she didn't want to be crazy, but because she wanted to see the woman again. She glanced at her watch. It was almost midnight. Krista had a thought and pulled her notepad from her pocket. She'd heard the "rats" for the first time just after midnight.

Maybe that was it. Afraid and anxious, she climbed onto the platform and approached the coffin. She knelt beside it, glancing up at the figure of the vampire hunter with the stake clutched in his hand. "What's it feel like to wake up every night staring up at that?"

"Frightening."

Krista shot a glance to the woman whose eyes were open, red light flashing in her pupils before it faded.

"You came back," the woman said, her voice soft and lyrical.

"I'm not some guy who pees his pants over a little thing like talking to a vampire."

The woman stretched her arms high and sighed. "It was nice. Waking up to see you instead of him," she said, wrinkling her nose at the figure poised above them both.

"What's your name?" Krista blurted, then felt heat creep across her cheeks.

"Mina. Yours?"

"Krista."

Mina held out her hand and Krista grasped it. The hand was cold, but warming fast inside hers.

"Let me help you up." Feeling clumsy, Krista straightened,

then reached out to help Mina from the coffin. Their gazes locked for a long moment. Then with her cheeks flushing a delicate rose, Mina stepped over the edge and hopped over the ropes to the floor. Not nearly as graceful, Krista followed. "I don't understand something."

Mina's chin lifted. "What do you want to know?"

"Last night. Time passed quick. One minute it's just after midnight. But then it's morning."

Mina walked around her, then leaned in from behind, her hands cupping Krista's shoulders. Her hair brushed the side of Krista's neck. Lips caressed her there.

"When I stood behind you yesterday," Mina whispered, "it wasn't just for a moment. I drank from you."

"Drank. As in you sucked my blood? Why didn't I feel it?"

"I wanted to linger. I bespelled you."

"Bespelled? As in, you cast a spell?"

"Not like a witch's chant, but more of a suggestion as I fed."

"Five hours' worth? You'd need a bigger straw."

Mina chuckled, her warm breath gusting against Krista's ear. "No. I did other things too."

"What other things?"

A gray blur whooshed around her. Mina stood close to Krista's chest. Her gaze fell. "I was curious about you." When she looked up, amusement glinted in her eyes. "I took out your notebook with your scribbles about rats."

"Reading that wouldn't take hours."

"I opened your shirt."

Krista's breath caught.

"When I pushed up the binding—"

"It's called a sports bra."

"When I pushed up the sports bra to see your breasts, I had to play with them."

"Was I a zombie while you did this?"

"You stood still, but you moaned when I touched you here," she said, rubbing a finger against her shirt. Right above her nipple.

The nipple sprang, beading tightly.

Mina plucked it with her fingers, then leaned closer and bit the tip poking through the cotton with her smaller, human-sized teeth.

Krista rocked on her heels, drawing a quick, sharp breath between pursed lips. "You couldn't have spent hours doing... that."

"There was more." Mina toyed with the waist of Krista's pants, tucking a finger inside the waistband and pulling her closer. "I pushed down your pants and your white panties. I tasted you there, then had to taste again and again. You came when I allowed it. Gasping. You cried when I finished. I bit you here," Mina said, rubbing a finger in the crease between thigh and labia.

"Now I know you're telling a story. I don't cry during sex."

Mina cocked her head and gave her a wicked smile. "You did for me."

Krista caught the hand rubbing between her folds and pulled it away. She stepped back. "You can't do that again."

The vampire clasped her hands together over her narrow waist. She cleared her throat. "Which part?" she asked softly. "Feed?"

Krista dragged in a deep breath, decision already made. "You can't make me forget."

Mina's features tightened. "But you would feel pain."

"I won't mind."

Mina shook her head. "You say that now."

"Again, I'm not some boy who's gonna pee his pants."

Mina's gaze dropped away.

"How often do you have to do that?"

"Feed?"

"Yes."

"At least once a week, or I get cranky," she said, with a crooked smile.

"Which is why the guards only lasted a week."

A dark winged brow arched. "You checked?"

"Of course. Not that I was sure any of this was real. But if it was, I wanted to understand. And now, since you denied me that knowledge…"

"You want me to take you now? Do it again, so that you know what you missed?"

Krista swallowed hard. "I don't want blood on my clothes."

Mina's pinched expression eased. "I wish we had a bed."

"The Marilyn exhibit—"

"Is in another hall. I can't leave this one."

"Why?"

Mina shook her head. "I just can't."

Krista blew out a deep breath as she thought about the problem. "There's a recliner in the employees' lounge. I'll be right back. You'll still be here?"

"I won't go anywhere. I can't."

Krista sped through the museum, marveling at the spurt of energy and her ease of movement. Her injury, for once, didn't consume her thoughts. She wrestled the brown vinyl chair onto a handcart and rolled it into Mina's hall. "If we keep it on the cart…"

"I understand."

Krista blinked and Mina was already sitting on an arm of the chair. She grinned. "I could get used to that."

"Looks like you have already." Mina patted the seat. "After you've undressed."

Well, Mina had already checked her out while she was zombified. Must not have been too disappointed. Krista shucked her utility belt, hanging it on a branch of the gnarled tree. She toed off her shoes, unbuckled her uniform trousers, then stripped off her shirt and pants. Standing in her underwear, she blew out a deep breath, then unsnapped her bra and let it slide down her arms.

Mina's gaze dropped to her chest, then lifted. Again, she arched a delicate brow.

The white panties went faster. She knew what she looked like. Tall, boyish athletic build with straight shoulders, a narrow waist and a small round bottom. A far cry from Mina's feminine curves.

Mina patted the seat again. "Sit that pretty little butt right here, Officer Pike."

The fake leather was cold under her cheeks, but the look in Mina's eyes as she slid over Krista's lap, straddling her thighs, melted her core. Hunger burned in Mina's dark gaze.

Mina went to work, pulling at the petticoats bunched between them until the last thin cotton layer was removed. Steamy, naked pussies aligned.

Mina leaned closer, her mouth so close to Krista's that her breath brushed Krista's lips like a caress. "Want something else to feel while I taste?"

Krista nodded, her tongue glued to the roof of her mouth.

Mina gave her a wicked smile, pulled the ruffled edge of her blouse below her breasts and tucked it into the top of her corset. Krista's mouth watered instantly at the sight of her ample breasts with their perfect pink areolas. The tips were just beginning to spike. Eagerly, Krista palmed them both, hefting the mounds, then sliding a thumb over the nubs. They were small, but growing harder.

Mina cupped the back of one of Krista's hands, trapping it against her. "Want it?"

"Yeah, I do. Right here in my mouth."

Mina let go and leaned over Krista, her hands flattening on the cushion at either side of Krista's head. She aimed her breast, rubbing the tip along Krista's lower lip.

Krista snaked out her tongue and lapped the swollen bead. Then she latched onto it, sucking it, pulling with her lips until Mina thrust her hand into her hair and held her there. She feasted on that warm, hardening nub, rubbing it, teething it gently. Then she backed away, staring at the reddened tip. "I want something, before you take that bite."

"Anything, Krista." Mina gasped and arched her back, rubbing her pussy on Krista's mound. "I'm feeling generous."

Krista reached for the lever at the side of the chair, raised the foot, then clutched the arms and pushed the back until it lay nearly flat. She scooted down, sliding beneath Mina. "I want you to strip, then turn around and put your pussy on my mouth."

"But we'll topple the chair."

"Not if you don't move too much. Balance yourself." She helped Mina strip away the layers of fabric, then turn. She held her hips while her round ass lifted and Mina scooted clumsily back.

The chair rocked. They both held still. Then Mina giggled. "I'll have to move lower."

"Lie down over me. Spread your legs wide—hang them over the sides if you have to. I want that cunt on my mouth."

The bottom in front of her face inched back. Mina's hands landed on Krista's knees, and she stretched out to distribute her weight. Mina spread her legs, and her pussy landed on Krista's chest.

Krista stuck her arms beneath Mina's thighs and tugged her

higher. Mina was spread, at her mercy, her pussy on Krista's chin. Krista slid her fingers in the creases between thighs and labia and rubbed up and down. The sex-slick lips parted, pulling the pink inner petals open, exposing her entrance. Krista ducked her chin and rubbed her lips all over the thickened outer labia, smoothing kisses north and south, nuzzling into Mina's sex to draw in her fragrant musk.

Krista's body was wound so tight, so hard. Her nipples ached and her sex was juicy and making lush, wet sounds. She scissored her thighs together, rubbing them and her labia. Then she eased them open beneath Mina, who was rubbing her cheek on her thigh.

"You can't bite. Not until I say so," Krista rasped.

"Who knew you'd be the mean one?" Mina dug her chin between Krista's folds.

Krista curved two fingers and thrust them into Mina while she licked at the bottom of her folds, lapping over the tiny hood. She twisted the digits, tunneling them inside, then pulling away, digging in again and again until Mina's buttocks tightened and her hips pumped up and down, giving Krista more sensory delight than she could stand.

She grabbed a buttock and pinched it, then smacked it with her open palm while continuing to lick and suck and thrust. Arousal seeped from Mina, and Krista licked it up, rubbing her tongue in the creamy film. She cupped four fingers together, curving them, then pushed them into Mina, who stiffened for a moment before undulating.

Mina's entire body shuddered. Her pussy gave moist, lewd caresses as it clenched around Krista's fingers. Mina sank deeper between Krista's legs to tongue her folds. The sounds, the heavy scent of Mina's steamy cunt, the feel of her from the inside—hot and raw and lush—pushed Krista over the edge.

She climaxed, giving a muffled cry. "Now, now, Mina!"

Sharp stings, like being gouged by an ice pick, halted Krista's orgasm. She bucked and writhed, trying to escape the bite, but Mina held firm, her hands pushing Krista's knees flat. Krista dug in her heels, vibrating against the pain, her head digging into the upholstery as she hissed between her teeth.

Mina'd sliced her on either side of her cunt, digging her fangs into the creases as she squeezed her thighs together, her lower jaw biting her labia, not piercing, but clamping to hold her still. Krista became aware of other sensations. Those lower teeth began to chew, gently. Lips suctioned against her, pulling her blood from other parts of her body, straight to her cunt in a thrilling, icy-hot rush. Her clit swelled, becoming achingly hard. A finger tapped it, then tapped it again—and just that quickly, Krista was there again, riding that roller coaster, taking the deep bend, then soaring high, pushing her pussy against Mina's mouth, begging her silently to take more and more.

But Mina disengaged, panting over her ravaged cunt.

Krista was breathing hard, her chest weighed down by Mina's ass, reminding her of the glorious gift parked an inch from her mouth. She licked her, cunt to asshole, a long wet slide of tongue that was followed by another and another until Mina keened and ground her pussy on Krista's mouth. Krista sucked Mina's clit, pulling on the tiny erect nub, pulling hard enough to stretch it and get her lips around the base. Then she didn't let go, teething it, licking the tip until Mina sobbed and quivered, stiffened, then slowly collapsed in a wet puddle.

"Hey. C'mon over here," Krista whispered.

Mina lifted her head, turned. Her eyes glowed red and stayed that way.

Krista should have been frightened by the wild, feral glance. Instead she opened her arms. When Mina snuggled against her chest, her nose nuzzling her neck, Krista didn't give a shit whether Mina took another bite to finish her or not.

There were worse things than dying.

Not having Mina again might be that one thing worse.

"So, explain why you can't leave this place," Krista asked Mina three days later.

Her lover stirred inside her arms, rubbing her cheek against her breast like a kitten rooting at her mother's teat. Her tongue gave the wet nipple beside her mouth another slippery swipe. "I'm trapped."

"By whom?"

"Your manager. Asshole has a grudge. And a terrible sense of humor."

Krista tugged a long lock of Mina's hair. "How can I help? How can I free you?"

"You've already done so much for me. I haven't been happier in forever." She sighed and slid her thighs to either side of Krista's hips, sliding deeper on the dildo Krista had strapped to the harness she'd worn beneath her uniform. A surprise that had delighted Mina no end.

Mina's blissful expression as she rocked forward and back didn't end Krista's inquiry. They'd spent aimless nights in each other's arms, but this night before Mina had awoken, Krista had been taunted with thoughts of more. She bracketed Mina's naked hips to halt her gentle motions. "How are you trapped?"

"I must sleep above the dirt I was buried in."

Krista's glance shot to the exhibit and the mound of dirt beside the deep grave.

"Not that dirt. He wouldn't make it that easy."

Krista forced Mina off her, ignoring the snarl and the flash of teeth. Mina liked to posture, and might well be vicious if provoked, but she liked it even better when Krista took charge.

Krista removed the dildo. "Sorry, babe. You're gonna have to do better than that. Show me."

They climbed onto the platform. Mina bent beside the pit and pointed toward the bottom. "Beneath that layer of dirt is a manhole. Beneath that is a welded grating. The dirt's under it, too deep to scoop it up."

Krista slid into the hole and tapped the bottom with her feet until she heard a hollow-sounding thud. She knelt and brushed away the dirt. The manhole was unremarkable. She lifted her chin to Mina. "I know you're strong. Get your ass down here and lift this."

Mina's mouth twisted, but she jumped over the edge, thrust a finger through the hole and pried open the heavy iron covering. Just as she'd said, a metal grate covered a deeper hole beneath it. Krista reached over the grave's edge for her utility belt, snagged her flashlight and shone it down into the hole.

"It's about six feet down."

Mina's shoulders slumped. "I told you, I'm trapped."

"Do you need all the dirt?"

"I need enough to sprinkle beneath whatever I'm sleeping on. Or I don't rest. And I can't move out of a twenty-five-foot radius of the dirt."

Krista nodded. "Put it back. We'd best clean up. It'll be dawn soon."

When they'd removed the traces of dirt from their bodies and dressed, Krista pulled Mina into her arms. "I'll figure something out."

The next night, Krista felt a tap on her shoulder.

"What are you doing?"

Krista pulled the long garden hose through the grating and

sat back on her haunches to wrap the hose around her arm. Then she laid it aside. She straightened, easing the ache in her hip, and climbed off the platform to stand beside the shop vac she'd duct-taped to the hose. "Want to take a walk?"

Mina cocked her head to the side, her gaze going from the hose to the appliance. "Problem solved?"

Krista unscrewed the top of the vacuum and pulled out the bag holding the dirt from the bottom of the hole. "I have a bed. Will you mind so much if I sprinkle a little of this under it?"

Mina's lips parted. Her eyes misted. "You did this for me?"

"I did this for us both—whether or not you come with me." She folded over the top of the bag, then handed it to Mina. "But now you have choices. You're free."

Mina reached for the bag, then pushed it back toward Krista. "I like it when you're in charge."

They made their way through the museum. At the door, Mina paused to read the note Krista had already taped there. Her laughter trilled.

Mr. Van Helsing—the rat problem is solved.

GEORGIA ON THE MIND

C.J. Harte

Growing up female in the Deep South is one big on-the-job training for a specific task: being a lady. It starts in the cradle and continues your entire life.

"Don't run, Georgia. It's not ladylike."

"No need to holler, Georgia. It's not ladylike."

"Georgia, get down out of that tree. It's not ladylike."

My granny, a feisty, white-haired terror of a Southern lady, treated even minor indiscretions with her favorite reminder. "Georgia, children and pets are cute. Horses and men are handsome. Ladies, well, dear, they are *ladies*. No further description needed." She then glared at me and continued in her no-nonsense tone. "Unless you are *not* a lady." Well, I knew I was a girl, but I wasn't sure I was a lady.

By my teens, my general answer was, "Hell, Granny, times have changed." Or maybe, "Damn it, Granny, I've heard it all before." This only added gasoline to an already flaming fire. This genteel, five-foot three-inch lady politely, but firmly scolded,

"Ladies do *not* use such language. And Georgia, by god, you *will* be a lady."

My mother, steeped in sweet tea, dusted with magnolia blossom and directed in the steps of righteous womanhood by my grandmother, was also a fine Southern lady. No further description needed. Mama took her Southern mother's role as a badge of honor.

"Georgia, you are my only daughter, but I assure you that doesn't relieve you of the obligation of being a lady."

Living up to this family tradition, however, was a challenge. Especially when I realized I was a Southern *lesbian* lady. After all, the women's movement had finally reached our little Georgia town and I was listening.

My coming out involved a lot of crying and talking among the females. The Southern family is a matriarchy. Once Granny and Mama realized this wasn't a phase, they just wanted to make sure that I could still be a lady. They were quite accepting. As long as I behaved like a lady.

I forgot everything the day *she* came into the store. *Damn, she's handsome* was the first thought that entered my head. I'm surprised I didn't say it out loud. And I certainly couldn't help but stare. Long, tan legs in khaki shorts. Tall, lean body that seemed just too delicious. Dark, short hair clinging to her head in this Georgia summer heat. She was a goddess.

She walked up to the counter and I prayed I wouldn't drool. That would definitely not be ladylike.

"Is there a car parts place around here?"

Her voice was smooth, like the water on the lake on a breezeless day, and just as refreshing. It was not the graceful *We'll get around to it in a minute* melody of the South. It was faster, to the point, and ignored the pleasantries of greeting and meeting. In these parts we refer to that as Yankee talk.

"Hello. You must be new around here or you would already know. Two blocks down to the red light and turn right. Go one more block. We have a garage if you need some car work. Right there on the corner." I found myself rambling but I couldn't stop. Every ounce of hormone in my body was on a rampage. "And there are a couple of people who do some work in their own garages. Tom Rankin and Rupert Smith are probably the two best, but Lonnie Carswell is the cheapest. Of course, Tom has been doing repair work for over twenty years. He moved to Atlanta and went to school there. Got a job at a big dealership. He got married, started having kids, then moved back here and opened his own place. That doesn't mean Rupert and Lonnie aren't good. Rupert worked with Tom for a while but he never was good at taking orders from other people. He..." She smiled and I got quiet. *Glorious heaven, she is handsome! And that smile...*

"Thank you," she said, and leaned on the counter. "Do you work for the automotive repair association?"

I looked into eyes so blue I thought I was looking into the sky on a clear Georgia morning.

"I just need an alternator."

"Well, the parts store probably has it. What kind of car you got?"

"It's a '75 Porsche. Usually runs smoothly. I can't part with it."

"Oh, my. I'm not sure we'd have a part. Our town's kinda small. Sometimes it's hard to get parts. Some folks go into Macon and buy Mercedes or Jaguars. Mostly the folks with money here. Doctors and lawyers. And people who made money off Coca-Cola. They've the biggest houses. Old money. Families worked for Coke when it started up and then settled here when they got rich. Wanted to get out of the city." I was rambling again. My heart hammering nearly as fast as my mouth. "Probably have to order a part for a ten-year-old car." This was not the information she wanted. "I'm sure they can order it and have it in a couple of days."

"A couple of days?" She slammed her hand on the counter. "Damn, I have to be in Jacksonville tomorrow."

I wonder if her granny ever talked to her about swearing.

She slammed the counter again. "Shit, I've got an interview."

I guess not. I looked at the hand and was awed by the strength. *So what if she does swear. Give me strength, dear Lord.*

"What kind of interview?" I really didn't care. I just wanted to stare at every inch of that tall drink of water, wishing her to stay here forever.

"For a job. Rental car company around?"

Sunshine had dropped into my life and was threatening to leave. I was not going to let it slip away...or her. "No need for a rental car. Everyone knows everybody. Only twelve hundred people. You can always find someone to carry you anyplace you want to go. Or sometimes folks have a second car and they let you borrow it. 'Course, sometimes, you get two or three people to give you a ride 'cause someone can drop you off in the morning and someone else picks up. Then if you need to run an errand, someone else—"

She put up her hand, sheer beauty in the smile on her face. *I'm dying.*

"I just need one car to get one person, me, to one city, Jacksonville. I can probably get one bus to come back and bring me to my one car."

She turned away. A dark cloud threatened. My mouth took a deep breath and plunged into potentially dangerous waters. "I'll take you!"

She turned and stared at me.

"I mean, if you want. I'm sure I can get a couple of days off." I went and stood next to her. I barely reached her shoulder. "My family owns the store and we kinda take turns. I've more turns lately because I've not had much to do. That's not right. I just have more flexibility in my schedule. I guess I don't have as much of a life as anyone else in the family. Well, I do but I don't have family obligations. I mean, I do but..." I'm offering to drive this woman to Jacksonville and she could be a serial killer. All I can ramble on about is my family!

She laughed. The room was lit with a thousand suns. "Do you ever answer anything in one word?" I started to answer but she again put up her hand. "If you're serious, I accept. How soon can we get started?"

"I'm serious. My mama and granny always told us to be careful about what we say. Even when we were little—"

"Good," she interrupted. "Can we leave soon? I need sleep tonight before the interview."

"I just need—"

"A simple yes-or-no question. Just nod yes or shake your head no."

I found my head bobbing up and down. I think I would have agreed to anything.

"Good. Sandra McKenna." She put out her hand.

"My name is Georgia Ann Rogers."

"Like the state?"

"Well, kinda. Actually I'm named after my granny and my mama. Granny is Georgia Louise and Mama is Georgia Lynn. I'm—"

"I get it." She shook her head. "No need to explain. Is there a wrecker service?"

I nodded. How wonderfully handsome she was. Actually,

this time the word was delicious. I had to lick my lips to keep from drooling.

"You can talk now."

Hope she doesn't read minds. I felt heat crawling up my neck.

"How do I get my car towed?"

"My brother, Bobby, can come get it. He helps out at the store sometimes. He's a sophomore at the college studying architecture. He's not sure if he wants to be an architect, but everyone in our family has to have a college degree. Bobby earns money by—"

"Georgia, how do I get my car towed?"

Determined to not embarrass myself any further, I quickly gave the necessary phone numbers. While she was making arrangements, I called my mama and told her a friend and I were going off for a couple of days. It was a white lie, but ladies were allowed to tell them...sometimes.

"Georgia, that's not very polite for her to just pop in and not stay for supper before carrying you off. You tell your friend that she has to sit a spell with us and at least have some tea."

"Mama, promise, we will when we get back." Short phone conversations were not possible in my family.

Mama was generally not too concerned when I went off with one of my college friends. Friends from Macon College were assumed to be from the right families. I just made sure we were not very specific about our plans.

Taking off with a stranger, however, was an entirely different matter.

"Georgia..."

I knew what was coming. "We won't be gone too long." I hung up before she could remind me to be a lady. It was our shortest conversation...ever.

* * *

The first ten minutes were excruciating. I'd rather spend the day at the dentist. Sandra was quiet and I was at a loss at what to say. Silence was as alien as a Florida Gator T-shirt. Old South culture demands a working knowledge of everyone's relations and how everyone is related. That certainly can't be done by quiet. "Where you from?"

"Ohio."

This was going to be a challenge. "Did you go to school in Ohio?"

"Yes."

"What school?"

She looked at me. Did she think I was crazy?

"Ohio State."

She was busy examining the landscape. I wondered if she was trying to memorize the route in case we got lost. I'd never met anyone who had so little to say. Growing up in Georgia, talking is more important than breathing.

"What did you study?" I was determined.

She continued to stare out the windows. "Pre-med. Medical school at Tulane. Internship and residency in New Orleans, and now I'm looking for a job. You?" She turned slightly in the car and it was easier for me to look at her. And to appreciate the goddess sitting next to me. "Wait, can you do this in twenty-five words or less?"

"Well, I've—"

"Yes or no." She laughed. The sound was so contagious I laughed.

"I don't know. Yes/no is only for when you're in trouble. When I was younger, my mama would ask me a question. I used to answer in one word. She would always say, 'Now, Georgia Ann, that's not enough answer, unless there is something you're hiding. If I want one word I will ask a yes/no question.' It was not polite to be so brief. One time my granny asked me about my school day and she made me sit for twenty minutes and tell her everything about everyone until she was sure she had heard about every minute of my day. I even had to—"

By now Sandra was laughing so hard she was wiping tears from her eyes. "I get it. Midwesterners, however, tend to be terse."

"You should see us at holidays when all the family gets together. Everyone talking at once."

She held up her hand. I now knew that meant stop talking.

"I just realized you haven't answered my question. Tell me about you. How long have you lived in Georgia? Have you always worked in the store?"

I thought carefully and tried to think of a short way to answer. I realized there was no one-word answer. "My family has lived in Georgia for over a hundred years. After the Civil War, my great-great-grandfather moved here from England to grow cotton."

Sandra's sigh was audible. I could feel her eyes burning through me. What was she thinking? Could I change for that woman? I could try.

"Land was cheap and we bought lots of land around here."

For the next fifteen minutes, I gave Sandra the shortened version of our history. Finally I brought her up to date. "I went to Macon College and majored in fine art. I have my own studio and hope to have my own exhibition some day."

"You're an artist?"

That Yankee voice was too much. Be still my beating heart. "A painter."

Sandra stared. "I think that is the shortest answer you've given me."

She smiled and I died. Well, at least, I just felt she had stolen a part of my heart...forever.

The six-hour drive flew by. Suddenly we were going through Savannah and I knew Jacksonville was not far. "Where are we staying tonight? I have some relatives who live near here. If we can find a phone…"

"Thanks." Sandra laughed. "I have a reservation not far from where I'm interviewing." She pulled some sheets of paper out of her bag in the back. "I have directions. Are we in Jacksonville yet?"

"No, ma'am. Another hour. This is Savannah. Can you smell that? That's the paper mill. I remember one time traveling through here…" I paused and recalled the first time my parents drove us through Savannah. I caught a quick glimpse of my passenger. Elegant profile. Strong chin with well-defined dimples. Dimples as deep as the Chattahoochee River. A classic nose. Skin that glowed. I wanted to paint her.

"Well, what happened?"

"Ma'am? Oh, well, uh…" There was a part of my brain that preferred looking to talking, but it's kind of hard to do that and drive. "Well, Mama didn't want to go because I had been sick. Dad thought the family should go together. As soon as we got near this town, I smelled the pulp mill and threw up all over the car."

"You feeling okay now?"

Oh, I'm wonderful. You're wonderful. And we would be even more wonderful together. That, however, was *not* a ladylike answer. "I'm fine."

"So we cross this river and we're in Jacksonville?"

I nodded. She planned out the shortest route to the hotel, and when we checked in it was already nine-thirty.

"I'm more tired than hungry," Sandra said, "but I'll go out for food with you if you're hungry."

"That's okay. You've paid for the gas and food. I just drove."

How sophomoric. She probably thinks I'm just a small-town hick. *Well, Georgia Ann, you certainly haven't demonstrated any great sense of Southern charm and intelligence.*

"You're a lifesaver. I can't miss this interview. I'm going to bed, then. I'll take a shower first." She grabbed some items out of her luggage, walked into the bathroom, and closed the door. I sat on one of the beds and realized I had packed only a few items—none of which were designed to sleep in. I decided my T-shirt would have to do. I stretched out on the bed and waited for Sandra to finish.

"Georgia. Georgia, wake up. We need to get ready for breakfast."

I had slept through the night. Fully clothed. Well, that took care of what to wear to bed. Now she *knows* I'm some small-town hick. I jumped up and headed to the bathroom.

I dropped Sandra off and we agreed I'd pick her up around two. The morning flew by. She climbed in and was smiling.

"Good interview?" I asked.

"Great. Got the job. Start next month. Enough time to go back, pack my stuff and move." She reached over and hugged me. "And I owe it to you."

If I died in the next five minutes, my life would be almost complete.

She leaned against the seat. "I'm taking you out to dinner. I've already gotten the name of a great restaurant."

I wanted to be happy for her, but a part of me secretly wanted her to move to Georgia. Well, Florida's not *that* far away. "I'm thrilled." I'm lying. This is not just a fib, or a little white lie, but a big bad lie. Definitely not ladylike. "I didn't interview for the store. I mean, I've almost worked there almost as long as I've walked. And all the family takes turns. So I didn't have to interview. I guess I haven't had to interview for anything."

Sandra just sat quietly.

"What was it like? I guess they asked lots of questions. And you had all the right answers. Of course they were impressed with how much you knew."

"Stop," she said. "Now you're talking for me. You're amazing."

An arrow shot through my heart. A sharp, tearing arrow. But when I looked at her she was smiling. "I guess I should apologize. It's not very ladylike to interrupt people. And my granny—"

"How does anyone in your family get a chance to talk?"

"Well, everyone talks and we just keep track of important things. My aunt Rachel one Christmas day started telling a story about some cousin and she didn't get finished until New Year's Eve. Good thing she was staying with us the whole time."

"You're pulling my leg?"

Thoughts of touching her leg, and other body parts, flowed deliciously through me, quickly raising my body temperature, even for a summer day. I turned up the air conditioner. "No, ma'am. It's the truth."

"God, it must be chaos."

I bet no one threatened to wash out her mouth. It was too yummy.

"Compared to your family, mine is noncommunicative. Let's go change and get something to eat." She reached for my hand. "I'll hear the rest of your story over dinner. I'm starving. How about you?"

Oh, Lordy, I was speechless. The touch of her hand warmed my skin and jolted my heart. The hunger I felt was not for food, but it would definitely be unladylike for me to say that out loud. I merely nodded. In all my life, short though it may be, never had any woman affected me as this one person. I don't think Granny or Mama would consider this ladylike.

We both quickly showered and changed. I put on a pair of navy blue cotton pants and a low-cut white lace blouse. I took a little more time than usual and hoped she'd notice. Suddenly it hit me. *What if she's straight?* I'd just driven how many miles with this incredibly attractive hunk of woman, allowed my fantasy to get the best of me, and she might not have any interest in me romantically. I struggled with my desire and my reluctance to let go of this dream. While she was still in the bathroom I changed my top to a pale blue button-down cotton shirt. I hope I hadn't made a fool of myself.

When she walked out of the bathroom, I didn't care.

She had on an off-white linen shirt that look tailored to fit her broad shoulders and tanned arms. A gold chain glittered around her neck. She wore black linen trousers that fit too well. She looked delicious. She was definitely on my menu.

"Ready?"

I struggled to control my mouth. My crotch was getting damp. *Ready? Oh, honey, I was born ready for you.* I nodded. It was the best I could do.

"Good! Mind if I drive? I've got the directions and I promise I'm a good driver."

I nodded. Southerners are always polite.

Sandra drove us to a charming seafood restaurant out at the beach. The atmosphere was casual and friendly. It was still light enough for us to watch the waves rolling in. "This is wonderful. I've never been here." I tried to keep the excitement out of my voice.

"Good. This will be a first for both of us." She raised her glass of wine and offered a toast. "To our first dinner together in Jacksonville."

Kerplunk! There went another piece of my heart. "I've been to Jacksonville lots of times and been out to eat. One of my cousins goes to school here. And I have lots of other cousins, aunts and uncles that live around here, from Yulee to St. Augustine and every place in between. We don't usually go out when we visit family because it is usually for family gatherings. I come down here with my friends sometimes, but mostly we go to Atlan—"

She leaned back in her chair and stared. "You know, one of the staff I met today is from Georgia and she talks just like you. Is that something you learn in the Georgia educational system?"

I felt chastised for unladylike behavior. My Georgia bulldog temper flared. "Miss McKenna, if you don't like the way I talk, I'll be quiet until we get you back. Besides, it is rude to make fun of one's heritage and upbringing. My granny..." I stopped. A warm hand rested on top of mine and electricity traveled through my body. Her touch shut down the thinking part of the brain.

"Georgia, I didn't mean to be rude. What I meant was I found it charming. It reminded me of you."

Her thumb stroked the top of my wrist. I definitely needed a change of underwear.

"Forgive me?"

Not if you keep doing that. She finally let go of my hand and I was again able to think. We chatted comfortably through dinner. I learned more about her family, friends and medical school. The more I heard, the more I liked. This was not good news.

After dinner, she asked, "How about taking a short walk on the beach so I can settle some of this feast?"

"Okay, as long as it isn't too far." The beach in front of the restaurant was mostly hard-packed sand. "My legs are like lead. My granny says that young ladies shouldn't take exercise after a big meal. I guess it's more a Southern thing."

"Not any exercise?" she asked.

There was something about her voice that set my pulse to racing. Was there hope?

She caressed my hand as we continued to walk. I kept hearing "kerplunk" with each stroke. Was any piece of my heart safe?

We walked a little farther and turned back. My heart was racing and, for once, it was faster than my mouth. She was doing all the talking. "Do you like to dance?"

I nodded. What else could a good Southern lady do in the face of a possible hurricane?

"Good. Some friends told me about a place."

When we got in the car, my stomach and heart had changed places. Supposed we ended up in some straight bar. This was my dream and I refused to let anything interfere. Then we pulled into the parking lot. *Ohmigod! A gay bar!*

"Hope you feel like dancing."

Sandra hopped out and opened my door. I was feeling light-headed. Inside it was early enough to find a place to sit. She asked, "What would you like to drink?"

"Coke with not much ice."

"Do you drink?"

"Sometimes. Not when I'm driving. My mama and daddy allowed us to sip wine and beer growing up so that we wouldn't be running off sneaking beer. They made sure that we knew to not drink and drive, though. Once my cousin Bud—"

She leaned down and kissed me. "Just hold it. Let me get something for us to drink because I have a feeling this will be a long answer." She smiled and then reached up and ran her fingers through my hair. My throat was dry and I could've drunk a gallon of Pepsi. Now, that would be unladylike.

The music was mostly fast. We danced some but, when a slow song came on, she took my hand. "Miss Georgia, may I have the pleasure of this dance?"

"My pleasure, Ms. McKenna."

I slid into her embrace and the rest of the world disappeared. She held me and I was in heaven. She led me gracefully around the floor. For the first time in my life, I truly felt like a lady in this wonderful woman's arms. The song ended too soon.

As we walked toward our table, she whispered, "Shall we go? I'm kind of tired."

"Yes," I answered breathlessly.

"Something wrong?" she whispered. "You only used one word."

"No, I'm fine." Liar, liar, pants on fire.

She took my hand and we walked to the car. We were silent the entire way. Inside I felt like Cinderella hearing the first clang of midnight. *Eleven more!* When we got to our room, I quickly changed into a T-shirt and climbed into my bed. Sandra went into the bathroom. The water from the shower was running. She was a doctor, I reminded myself, and I was just someone from a small town. It would be easier to control Niagara Falls than the tears threatening to wash down my face. How could she be interested in me? After all, I'm not very ladylike.

"Georgia? Georgia, are you awake?"

I was now. She was lying on the bed next to me. "I wasn't really sleeping. Just kind of resting my eyes."

She chuckled and stretched out next to me. "Do you have a girlfriend?"

I was as nervous as a June bug on oily water. If I said yes she might think I was off-limits. Of course, she could be one of those women who preferred playing around with unavailable women. If I said no, she would know I was available but maybe wonder what was wrong with me. Sometimes I wondered the same thing. I mean, I'd had a couple of girlfriends but none since I had moved home. When you live in a small town, there may not be too many choices. And too many of the folks are kin anyway.

"Georgia, this is a yes-or-no question. Unless you prefer boys."

Ohmigosh. "No, ma'am. I mean no, I don't like boys. I mean I do. I have three brothers. And I like them, but only as brothers. Except for the ones that aren't brothers. I mean, they're okay for friends—"

"Georgia! Do (pause) you (pause) have (pause) a girl-friend?"

"No. I mean, it's not because I haven't had girlfriends. That is, I have. You know, like as in girlfriend girlfriend, but in my town the pickings are slim and I've tried to focus—"

A kiss halted further explanation. It was the most wonderful kiss.

"You are the most exasperating person, Georgia Ann Rogers, and the most charming. Now let me crawl under the covers and hold you." And she did. It didn't take long for me to fall asleep with those arms wrapped securely around me. My heart had found a home.

"Georgia. Come on, Georgia, wake up."

My dreams were about a young dark-haired physician. As I opened my eyes I was confronted with reality. A young dark-haired physician. "What time is it?"

"It's nearly eight o'clock. I waited as long as I could. It was fun watching you sleep, but I'm hungry."

"No, I'm sorry. I'm usually up by now."

"I want to buy breakfast." She smiled and my world tilted. "Then we head back and I pick up my car."

My world returned to its usual flattened state. I swallowed my disappointment and rapidly dressed. As we crossed the state line, I searched for any excuse to hold on to this woman.

"My mama's expecting you to have supper with us when we get back."

"That's nice, Georgia, but I don't know your family."

"That's okay. I told her you were a friend of mine, and that's all that matters. In small towns everybody knows everybody, and if you're a friend or relative then you're already welcome. Besides, Mama wants to make sure she knows all my friends. She's always trying to play matchmaker. One time my friend—"

"Matchmaker? She knows you're gay?"

"She caught me kissing my best friend in high school. I thought I'd never hear the end of it. She went on for days. Actually, she was more worried that I might not behave like a lady. Now she just wants me to be happy. One time I brought my friend Julia home from college. She was a very close but straight friend. Unfortunately my friend didn't know about me, and Mama started asking about her intentions. Well, my friend Julia thought she was asking about her major. So Julia's talking about business classes. Contracts and negotiations, and Mama's talking about wedding plans. It was the funniest conversation. On the way back, Julia told me she thought my mama was really nice. My cousin Sammy's mother's just as bad..." I looked over and saw Sandra smiling. "What?"

"Miss Georgia, I would love to have dinner with your family."

I decided to ignore the chimes of the clock tolling. I would enjoy whatever time we had together. And I did what I knew best. I talked and was a lady.

EXOTIC MASQUERADE

L.T. Marie

I glanced in the mirror, finally satisfied with the outcome. The small amount of mascara I'd applied to my eyelashes enhanced my deep blue eyes. Securing my blond hair into a ponytail with a clip helped expose the sides of my neck. My friends explained that the more skin I displayed tonight, the better, for this would be a new experience for me. Tonight I would be attending my first Exotic Masquerade Ball.

The black number I'd bought for the special occasion was strapless and seemed to hug my curves in all the right places. The dress was far from what others would be wearing, or better yet, not wearing. I was going more as an observer, not expecting more than a passing glance. Feeling comfortable enough with my sexuality to parade around half-naked would never be an option. I harbored some lingering self-consciousness after being the brunt of some unkind remarks when I was younger. Being a chubby kid with braces didn't do much for my self-esteem. Was I popular as I grew older? Prom queen? Nope. It took me until college to come out of my shell. To gradually accept the person I saw every day in the mirror.

This evening, though, wouldn't be about me. Tonight was about the thousands of others, showing off their bodies in many festive and unusual ways. I'd been anticipating the event for weeks. My friends said it would be a night I'd not soon forget.

From all the literature regarding the festivities, the ball was a mixture of Mardi Gras, a burlesque show, and a rock concert all bundled up in one delicious package. Those who did wear clothes wore very few. Leather, lace, garters and see-through material were all popular combinations. Then there were those who decided to go naked as the day they were born. Shyness was not an issue. These people paraded around letting it all hang out, literally. Some would spice up their bodies by using paint, or place a piercing in a not-so-practical place. But who was I to judge? They were there to express their sexual freedom and I, for one, was going to help them celebrate by admiring their candidness.

As the cab pulled into the pavilion, crowds of people were already spilling out onto the streets. Everyone seemed to be in a good mood. They had drinks in their hands and posed for the hundreds of cameras that were firing off in rapid succession. The flashbulbs from the cameras were already affecting my vision and I figured by the time I made it through the doors, I was going to be either famous or blind.

I made my way up the staircase and leaned on the railing above the bustling crowd. The clock chimed nine P.M., still too early for the thousands more who would arrive throughout the evening. The costumes were more spectacular than I could have imagined. People of all shapes and sizes adorned the large room. Stages set up for the many different scenes that would be played out over the course of the night filled the corners of the extravagant ballroom. In one corner, three muscular men were posing like Greek statues, black cowboy hats covering their intimate parts. A few curious onlookers stood directly below them, peering up at the Adonis-like specimens, hoping to get a glimpse of those parts. If the objects of interest matched the rest of their impressive bodies, I was positive those onlookers would be quite pleased.

In another part of the room, two men dressed as storm troopers from *Star Wars* had a woman wearing a thong and two star pasties barely covering her rose-colored nipples bent over between them. She appeared to be giving one of them a blow job while the other pumped his hips into her ass from behind. I admired their creativity, but that scene wasn't the one currently holding my attention.

A blond woman in a leather bustier that tied down the center of her chest and exposed much of her breasts had been chained against the far wall, her legs spread-eagled. A handsome butch crouched between her thighs, seemingly intent on biting her way through the restrained woman's red thong. I was fixated. This was truly one of the most erotic things I'd ever witnessed.

The blonde threw her head back and closed her eyes. Even though I couldn't hear her over the noise of the crowd, I knew she was groaning by the subtle way her lips twisted. The brunette between her legs started nibbling at the ties that held the bustier together. I was wet and my nipples hardened in reflex. My mind began to play tricks on me and suddenly I became the chained woman. Their scene had me so mesmerized, I didn't register the person standing behind me. When arms slipped around me and hot breath tickled my neck, I nearly came.

"Like what you see?" the deep melodious voice whispered before a tongue carefully rimmed my earlobe.

"Who are—"

"Shh. I've been watching you since you arrived. I see what you see."

I wanted to turn around, but instinct told me that wasn't how this scene would be played out. I was no expert, but from what I had already witnessed, tonight was not about the knowing. Tonight was about the mysterious. The unknown.

The arms that circled beneath my black tuxedo jacket were strong and firm. The long, tan fingers promised passion beyond my comprehension. When I could focus again on the scene, the leather-clad brunette was running her thumb firmly against the red silk between the bound woman's legs. I imagined the strong fingers that now gripped my wrists doing the same to me. I bit my lip to stifle a moan.

"What is your name?" the stranger asked.

"Angel."

"Angel." She moved closer, crushing me to her body. "What is your pleasure this evening?"

"I came to watch."

"Just watch?"

She ran a single finger up my arm and dipped the digit between my breasts. When she grazed my right nipple, it shot to attention. "Yes."

"Then watch."

Focusing on the two women below was becoming impossible as the heat between us melted any resistance that I thought I had. I could never recall wanting anyone so much in my life. "I can't watch."

"Why not?"

"My attention seems to be elsewhere."

She slowly turned me in her arms and I gazed up into dark, penetrating eyes. She was a good three inches taller than my own five foot five, and her long legs instinctively molded to mine. Her black Venetian Mardi Gras mask with gold detail highlighted the almost imperceptible flecks in her eyes. She was captivating. Sexy beyond words.

"Tell me?"

The question didn't make sense at first—I was too caught up in the way her lips moved to comprehend anything she was saying. The inability to see more of her face caused my insides to tingle. My clit throbbed and I wasn't just wet anymore. I was soaked.

"You. My attention is on you."

"Come with me?"

For the first time since our encounter, I sensed a bit of uncertainty in her touch. When I squeezed her hand in answer, her hesitation vanished like the proverbial rabbit in a hat. I followed wordlessly, her hand tugging gently on mine. This was not what I had expected tonight, to be swept off my feet by a stranger. But swept was what I was as we climbed into a cab and headed downtown to my hotel.

She never removed her mask as we made our way up the elevator to the tenth floor. Tonight was the night of masquerade. Tonight was Halloween.

She followed close behind as I led her down the hall. My room was at the end, and the never-ending walk vibrated with nervous anticipation. When I opened the door to my hotel room, the gravity of the situation caught me by surprise. I hesitated and she bumped into my back. I was immediately assaulted by a mixture of musk and a hint of spice. Her breathing had subtly changed, and the pulse point thudding wildly in her neck was a sure sign her restraint was wavering. She pulled me closer, her lips inches from mine.

"Why me?" I asked as she bent her head and drew me closer. There had been so many beautiful women there tonight and I wanted—*needed*—to know why this handsomely attractive stranger chose me.

"Because you were the hottest woman in that room. From the moment I saw you, I ached to touch you. To feel you."

That did it.

Instantly, I went from a reserved ball of mush in this woman's arms to a person consumed with lust and fiery passion. I took her lips in an all-consuming kiss, driving her backward onto the bed. Straddling her slim hips, I looked down into her soft, dark eyes. They were cloudy and out of focus. I didn't remove the mask. She was my mystery lover and I wanted to remember her this way for the rest of my life. As I leaned forward to kiss her, she wrapped her arms around my waist, picked me up, and deposited me on the chair near the bed.

My head spun when she spread my legs and pushed my dress up around my hips. I watched her thumb massage my clit through my black lace panties and shivered at the familiar scene. I had been wrong earlier. The two women from the Masquerade Ball had excited me, but *this* was the most erotic thing I had ever witnessed.

She pressed harder as a groan escaped my lips, her thumb moving in no apparent rhythm. My clit throbbed—those knowing hands holding me hostage without the need for restraints. When she pinched me gently through the soaked material, I was primed and ready to burst.

"Please..."

"Tell me what you want," she whispered, her warm breath tickling between my thighs. She wet her lips and released me as I gasped.

"Put your hands back on me."

"Just my hands?" She pulled my panties tighter over my clit and began massaging me with her tongue. I could feel myself swell under the silk material. The twin sensations of silk and warm muscle were too much. I cried out.

"You taste incredible," she said, swiping her tongue once more over my engorged flesh. I buried my hands in her short dark hair, silently requesting that she not leave that position anytime soon. She must have recognized the gesture, because the next time her tongue passed my throbbing lips, she slipped it under the material. I thrust my hips forward to meet her.

"Please…no more teasing."

"What do you want?" she repeated, her voice thicker this time, desperate with need. Her breathing had become more erratic. She was holding back. She was the one figuratively wearing the restraints. I released her.

"Fuck me."

She painstakingly slid the panties off my hips and down my legs, following their retreating path with her tongue. The return journey was even slower, but when she buried her face between my legs, she lapped at my clit like a parched person in need of water. I wiggled in the chair, trying to hold off the orgasm that was surfacing with each pass of her talented tongue. When she took me between her lips and sucked, I thought I was going to fly off in a million directions.

"Yes! Oh, god, yes!"

The orgasm rocked me hard into her mouth and she took me more fiercely, my hips pumping into her face as she drove me relentlessly to a second and then a third orgasm. Just the sight of her feasting between my thighs brought wave after wave of intense pleasure.

"No more," I pleaded as I felt her smile against my wet lips. But just as the waves began to recede, she pushed into me hard with a quick thrust of her fingers. She stood, her hand inside me, as I wrapped my legs firmly around her waist, accepting each thrust with an answering surge of my own. Heat engulfed me as she strummed her thumb along my clitoris, and orgasm raced along my spine. She held me tightly as I fell limp into her arms. The soft kiss she placed upon my lips was the last thing I registered before my body gave in to sleep.

I awoke the next morning to find that my mystery woman was gone. The thought saddened me and there was no way to hide my disappointment. I was pleasantly sore but satisfied beyond my comprehension. My legs felt like Jell-O, but I managed to stand and caught a glimpse of a familiar object sitting on the dresser. The mask sparkled as if calling out to me. A single red rose, a gift to let me know she was real. I picked up the note, my mystery lover's scent evident on its cream colored paper. My hands shook.

Beauty is in the eye of the beholder.

The knowledge that this woman had seen in me what I always failed to see in myself made me smile. I clutched the note to my chest and closed my eyes. My night had come to an end, but I would remember it—and her—always.

As I dressed in my usual attire, I ran my hand along the black dress that had captured the eye of the most beautiful woman in the room. Even though I never saw her face, I felt her soul through her gentle touches. To succumb to her power still made me shiver. For one amazing night I had attracted the most exquisite woman in the room, but now it was time to return to my ordinary life.

I checked out of the hotel and stopped in their café to have a coffee and croissant before heading home. The morning newspaper was loaded with images from last night's events, and just as I prepared to leave, a gentle hand gripped my shoulder from behind.

"Good morning, my Angel," my wife, Jase, said as she bent to kiss me below my ear. She took my hand in hers, the fingers I knew so well after ten years of marriage igniting my passion effortlessly.

"Hello, baby. How was your evening?" I asked as she rounded the table and took the seat across from me. Her dark chocolate eyes bored into mine, lust and love mingling in her stare.

"Very mysterious. And yours?"

I smiled as I brought the cup of coffee to my lips. "Let's just say that for one magical night, I was the belle of the ball."

THE BUCKET LIST

Charlotte Dare

I knew I was in love with Ellie that morning in New York City as we sat together, bumping along in the back of an air-conditioned cab. It was a month after "the kiss" and she still wanted to be friends—a good sign. She smelled so good, clean and fresh from some Bath & Body Works lotion girly-girls wore, and perpetually minty from constant refills of Mentos chewing gum. As she rambled about loving jaunts to the City, I realized everything I ever wanted was right beside me. I watched her shiny cranberry lips move as she spoke, but all I could think about was the kiss several weeks back, the number two item on my bucket list that Ellie had helped me cross off. Sweet and sensual, that kiss was still as palpable as if it had happened only a minute earlier.

When she finished praising New York for its culture and sophistication, she looked ahead at the snarled traffic and grimaced. "I don't know how people can live here."

"I couldn't do it," I said, still studying the curve of her soft face. Her delicate antique earrings danced from her lobes each time we hit a pothole.

"Stop staring at me," she growled with half a smile. "I hate it when you stare at me like that."

"I'm not staring," I said. "I'm just looking. Not my fault you're cute."

"Oh, yeah, right." Like always, she dismissed my compliment as though I were a used-car saleswoman on the last day of the quarter. "What time does the curtain go up?" She knew very well we had tickets for a one o'clock matinee of *Mamma Mia!*

Looking back, asking my unavailable friend if she wanted to be my Number Two was an extraordinarily stupid thing to do, but my attraction to Ellie since she and her partner bought the condo unit next to mine two years ago had become unmanageable by late spring. I was starting to say and do stupid things with alarming frequency.

I sneaked another peek at her profile as she kept her eyes peeled for every car and bus our driver nearly sideswiped along Forty-second Street. Ellie was fifty-seven, but her smooth Mediterranean skin, Bambi-brown eyes and youthful enthusiasm made her ageless to me.

"Can I have a sip of your coffee?" she asked.

I handed her the cup and stuck my hand into a white paper bag containing the cinnamon streusel I'd bought earlier at Grand Central Station. I bit into the warm, moist cake and grinned at her, my lips coated with cinnamon sugar. "Wanna kiss me?" I asked, assuming she would laugh it off as innocent flirtation. To my surprise and hers, she leaned over and pressed her lips against mine, grinning back at me as she licked the sweet mixture from her lips.

"That's hot," I joked. Although I was playing it cool, that kiss sent a jolt of tingles through my entire body.

"I know," she confessed, reapplying her lipstick. "I've been thinking that since June."

I nearly choked on the streusel. "What do you mean?"

"What do you mean, *what do I mean?*" She grew flustered, trying to downplay her comment by picking lint off her black capri pants. "I told you I liked it right after it happened."

"I know you did, but I had no idea you've been thinking about it since June."

She rolled her eyes and turned toward her window.

I was more than shocked. I'd had a fantasy of being with an older woman since I was a teenager, but by thirty-eight, I had all but abandoned hope of it ever coming true. Ellie was older and beautiful, but in a relationship. I had considered myself lucky when she'd consented to the bucket list kiss that night on my balcony after a couple of glasses of Merlot.

"Ellie, are you trying to tell me something?" I gently patted my highlighted spikes to make sure they hadn't fallen victim to the humidity.

"Honestly, Suzanne, I don't know. I don't know what I'm saying. Did I enjoy the kiss? Yes. Do I want to kiss you again? Yes, but am I going to? No. I'm in a relationship, first of all, but I also really love our friendship and don't want to ruin it."

We got out of the cab at Forty-sixth Street so we could grab a quick bite to eat before the show. We continued the discussion strolling up Broadway toward Rockefeller Center in the heavy air.

"Then why did you kiss me in June?" I asked after taking a few minutes to process the unreality of the conversation.

"I don't know," she snapped. "I thought it would be fun to be on your bucket list, something wild and silly. You know how I am. I never ever imagined it would actually turn me on." She shook her head. "And I'd keep thinking about it for weeks afterward. I've been with Cheryl for over fourteen years."

"You also said it's been a long time since things felt right."

She sighed heavily. "We've really been trying to make it work. She's been talking about retiring from the hospital and doing part-time, in-home care."

I remained quiet, rubbing at the last spot of streusel stickiness on my finger as we walked.

"Look, Suz, it's never gonna happen for us," she said. "So let's not talk about it anymore and just enjoy the afternoon together."

Her angst charged through me like I was a lightning rod. "You don't have to get all worked up about it. I'm sorry I kissed you in the cab. I promise I won't ever bring up the subject again."

She grabbed my arm and stopped before we approached a hot dog vendor. "You didn't kiss me in the cab. I kissed you. And I want to kiss you again. That's why I'm getting all worked up."

"Shit," I whispered to myself. I felt like a total schmuck for joking with her about my bucket list in the first place. She had a partner. What was I thinking? But then who ever thinks a fantasy is really going to come true?

I ordered us two dogs with the works, and we slapped each other's hands away as we both waved our money at the vendor. "Will you let me fucking pay for this," Ellie said. "You get the cab back later."

She took a huge bite of her hot dog and absorbed the Manhattan skyline, intentionally avoiding eye contact.

After several minutes of silence, I said, "Ellie, can I be honest with you?"

She exhaled deeply. "Please do."

"I would love nothing more than to kiss you again. It's all I've been thinking about since it happened—a heck of a lot more than you, I'm sure. But our friendship means the world to me, and I don't want to ruin it either."

"This is so crazy. I'm nineteen years older than you. What do you even see in me?"

"It's probably the last thing you want to hear right now, but you're everything I want in a woman—I just love being with you. You're fun, sexy, so pretty and most of all, you get me."

She smiled, her brown eyes sparkling above the rims of her DKNY shades. "But I'm not single."

"I know."

She grabbed my Diet Coke and sipped from my straw. "And too fucking old for you."

We laughed and, in unspoken agreement, savored the rest of our day in New York as friends, with no further mention of bucket lists or secret desires.

After our excursion to the city revealed more than we'd both intended, Ellie avoided me for a good two weeks—six days in New Hampshire visiting her daughter and grandson made it easy for her, but it made me a wreck thinking she'd washed her hands of the whole sordid situation. By the second week, I was missing her like crazy, convinced she was scheming to find a diplomatic way to end the friendship so I wouldn't go all Glenn Close on her ass. If it was true, I would survive, even though the thought of losing her as a friend crushed my heart. But I was a butch after all—I didn't chase down hot femmes, they chased me.

When Ellie finally texted *Found a great new Chardonnay*, I flew downtown to the gourmet shop for the perfect comple-ments to her wine selection. Okay, so we would be friends and nothing more. Fine with me. As I prepared the bistro table on my deck with Brie, horseradish cheddar, crackers, grapes and citro-nella candles, my stomach fluttered. *Are you serious*, I thought.

Butterflies, clammy palms? This wasn't a date—it was just Ellie and our regular Wednesday night wine tasting-slash-bitch fest.

The first glass of wine went down quickly and easily for both of us. No cheese chaser or fruit accompaniment, just straight down and into the bloodstream. A few sips from our second, and we were back into the familiar terrain of relaxed girl talk. As cool as I played it, inside I was dying. She looked more beautiful than ever, her cheeks shiny and bronzed from the sun.

"I hope you're not still feeling weird about New York," Ellie said. "I'm not."

"Neither am I."

Liars.

"Good," she said, her legs bobbing on the edge of the wrought-iron bistro chair.

"So I bet Cheryl will be glad to give up these night shifts when she retires." The selfish bitch in me wondered how it would impact my time with Ellie.

She nibbled a slice of cheddar pensively. "She has seniority. She could've given them up a long time ago."

"Why didn't she?"

She gave me her famous *Duh* look. "Let's just say it was better for the relationship when we weren't together constantly."

"I can't imagine anyone not wanting to be with you constantly."

"You know how it is. You were with Angie for eleven years."

I studied her gorgeous, softly aging face and that sensual bottom lip I daydreamed of biting on numerous occasions. "And I knew things weren't right with us. That's why we're not together anymore."

"Well, you're young. You shouldn't stay in an unhappy relationship."

"But if you're old, you should?"

"I didn't say that, and I never said I was unhappy with Cheryl."

"You never said you're happy with her either."

"Suz, you're still so young. You don't understand."

I shook my head at her stubbornness and leaned back in my chair.

"I don't think I've ever been as happy as I am when I'm with you," she said quietly.

The butterflies returned in a swarm on that one. Maybe it was my empty-stomach wine buzz or just wishful thinking, but I swear I caught her checking out my chest as I stretched. Maybe she was just reading the Ed Hardy logo on my black tank top.

"These mosquitoes are terrible tonight," she said. "Should we go inside?"

"Sure, we can if you want." I downed the rest of my wine like a shot.

We got up in unison to gather the bottle, glasses and snacks and take them into my living room. As she reached across me to grab the cheese knife, I stuck my nose in her hair and moaned at the sweet coconut scent of her shampoo.

"What are you doing?" she asked with a smirk.

"Nothing. What are *you* doing?" *Son of a bitch*, I thought. What the hell was wrong with me? My heart was racing just standing near her, and now we were heading to my couch. I followed her through the sliders, watching her ass as she went inside.

"I think you better slow down and eat something," she said over her shoulder.

"And ruin this nice buzz?"

We arranged the food and drink on the antique chest that doubled as my coffee table. I sat in a chair as Ellie curled up in the center of the couch. She shot me a look. "What are you doing over there? Afraid of me now?"

I giggled. "Why would I be afraid of you?"

"The dirty old lady says she wants to kiss you again and suddenly, you're sitting clear across the room."

I stood up and poured myself another glass, my hands shaking to match the rest of me. "As I recall, you said it's not going to happen again, so what difference does it make where I sit?"

"Fine." She pursed her lips and absently played with the strands of hair falling out of her hair clip. "Sit wherever the hell you want, but you better eat something. I think you're getting sloshed."

"Fine. I'll eat something." I plunked down next to her on the couch and made a pepperoni and cheese cracker sandwich, stuffing the whole thing in my mouth.

The setting sun burned red through my sliders. She gently bounced the edge of her wineglass off her lip as she returned my gaze, and I was jealous of the lipstick print her mouth left on the rim.

"Here, have some of these," Ellie said and shoved a few grapes in my mouth.

Her middle finger was warm as it brushed over my lips. I closed them around her finger for a second, expecting her to yank it back. She didn't. Instead, she slid it across my bottom lip and then tasted it.

My clit erupted into wild pulsations as we stared into each other's eyes, her breathing suddenly shallow and quicker. My mouth watered at the thought of tasting her tongue again, the sweetness of her full tits, her pussy as I would explore it slowly, gently with my mouth.

"Would you get mad at me if I kissed you?" I whispered, my lips inches from hers.

She smiled with her eyes, shook her head almost imperceptibly. I took her hand in mine and it was trembling. She looked down, suddenly shy.

I leaned in and kissed her, gliding my lips across hers, lightly flicking my tongue around her mouth. She moaned, scooped my face in her hands, and kissed me harder, sucking my lips till I tasted the fruit she'd eaten.

"Suz," she whispered through kisses. "I can't stop thinking about you, and not just about kissing you. I can't fucking sleep at night."

"What are you thinking?"

She didn't answer, but she didn't have to. I gently nudged her back against the cushioned arm of my couch and slipped my tongue deep into her mouth. She wrapped her legs around my waist, her arms around my torso and squeezed, digging her fingers into my back.

"I keep thinking about you making love to me, and it makes me so horny. I shouldn't be feeling this way, but I can't stop. I'm such an awful person."

"I'm sorry, Ellie. Just tell me if you want me to stop."

"But I don't want you to," she whimpered.

I slipped my hand up her shirt and caressed her butter-smooth side, running my hand over her pelvic bone and down to her ass. She was breathing hard, kissing me harder as my fingers found her nipples poking up from her firm breasts. I twisted them as she devoured my lips, refusing to let go of my face. Her tongue twirled around mine as my hand worked its way into her pants, sliding over her bush and into her wet pussy.

"Oh, my god," she moaned as I rubbed her swollen clit, slowly up and down, savoring her slick velvet against my fingers. Her legs opened wider, her body moved in rhythm with my hand as my fingers spread out across her pussy, caressing her lips as my middle finger steadily worked her clit.

"Mmm, you're gonna make me come," she whispered, tightening her grip on my shoulders.

I stopped fingering her, intending to finish the job with my tongue, but she grabbed my hand and shoved my fingers back into her pussy. "No, don't stop. This feels so fucking good."

I pressed into her more firmly and stroked her slowly, all around, faster as she pumped her pelvis into my hand. She clung to me, panting in my ear, her climax building slowly, torturously, until it rocketed her into orgasm.

"Oh, shit, Suz," she breathed. "Oh, god, that was so good. I can't believe it."

"I can't either." I kissed her gently on the forehead. "Maybe you'll sleep better tonight."

She exhaled deeply. "Or it's gonna be even worse." Snaking her arm around the back of my head, she pulled my mouth onto hers and licked my lips. "I wanna taste you so bad." She pushed me off her and back against the other sofa arm and was on me with the urgency of Cinderella at ten to midnight.

"Are you sure you want to—" Before I could finish the sentence, she ripped open my cargo shorts and dragged my black Calvins down to my ankles.

Her warm tongue on my throbbing clit was welcome relief as her hands roamed under my tank top, around my bare stomach, reached for my tits, pinched my nipples. After teasing me gently with her tongue, she found the spot and moved in for the kill, eating my pussy until I was shuddering in ecstasy.

We held each other until our bodies settled and then cuddled for what seemed like hours after. Ellie nuzzled up closer under my arm and whispered, "How did this happen?"

I brushed her bangs out of her eyes. "I hope it happened because we both wanted it to."

She looked up at me and smiled, her beautiful brown eyes sleepy with satisfaction. "You certainly didn't force me." She sat up and began fixing her disheveled clothes. "It was a wonderful experience, but it won't happen again. I'm sorry." Glancing into the mirror behind the couch, she raked her fingers through her hair.

"You mean like the bucket list kiss?" I felt bad after I said that, but the determination in her voice stung.

"This is different, Suzanne."

"But I know you'd rather be with me."

She glared at me. "This isn't only about Cheryl. I'm almost twenty years older than you."

"That doesn't matter to me."

"It should. I had breast cancer."

"I know, and you survived."

"The point is it could come back. I'm almost fifty-eight years old. You're thirty-eight. I'd never put that on you."

"There are lots of people my own age who've had cancer. Should I not date them either?"

"Suz, you're not getting it. I'm too old for you, and I just couldn't leave Cheryl now. She's sixty-two years old. What's she supposed to do if I come home one night and say, 'Hey, guess what, I'm leaving you for someone twenty years younger'?"

Fearing my eyes couldn't contain the deluge of tears threatening to burst forth, I got up and switched on a light in the corner of the living room. "Thanks for killing the afterglow. Care for a bottled water?"

"No thanks. I should get going." She walked over to me and took my hand. "Suz, I really had an amazing time with you tonight—but I always have an amazing time with you. That's why we can't do this again."

I squeezed her hand. "I'm sorry if I did anything to make you feel uncomfortable."

"You didn't." She smiled as she studied my face for a moment. She said good night and leaned in for a gentle peck on my lips.

"Good night." I let her leave without incident despite my desire to throw my arms around her and beg her to leave Cheryl.

The days and weeks after our night of passion were torture. With all the preaching and proselytizing about how we couldn't ruin our friendship, we'd still managed to fuck it up thoroughly and in record time. No matter how hard I tried to forget Ellie, I just couldn't. Something about her made it impossible. But what could I do? She belonged to someone else. If I was destined to languish on Lonely Street for all eternity, it was a penance well deserved, but I knew I couldn't do it living next door to her for much longer.

Autumn came and went, and I was slowly going crazy alternately obsessing about Ellie and then browbeating myself for still wanting her. On the Monday morning after New Year's, I crunched across the frozen parking lot carrying the garbage to the Dumpster before work.

Ellie caught me as I headed to my car. "I saw the paper yesterday," she said.

"Happy New Year to you, too." As much as I desperately wanted to drag her into my car and drive us far away, I opted for ambivalence, aided by bone-chilling air that kept my face naturally stoic.

"Why did you put your place on the market?" she asked, wrapping her arms around herself and rubbing her arms.

I stood my ground at my open car door. "Why does it matter to you? You haven't spoken to me in months."

"Not to make an issue of it, but you haven't talked to me either."

"Not to make an issue of it," I mocked, "but you have a

partner and made it abundantly clear that wasn't going to change."

"Well, it has—right before Christmas, as a matter of fact."

"What do you mean, you broke up with her?"

She hugged herself tighter against the cold. "I didn't have to. When Cheryl asked me why I never seemed happy anymore, I broke down—completely. She just knew."

"About us?"

Ellie shook her head. "That it was time to let go."

"How is she? Is she all right?"

"She will be, we both will."

"Well, if you ever want to talk over a glass of wine, friend to friend, let me know."

"Suz, I just can't be your friend."

Although I had made peace with our situation a while ago, hearing her say those words was like catching a snowball with my face.

"I can't be just your friend 'cause I'm in love with you," she continued. "I need us to be more. I've needed it since the first time you kissed me." A smile tickled the corner of her mouth.

The breath I'd been holding for months billowed out into the crystal air. "You should come over tonight. I have a great Riesling chilling."

Ellie smiled wide through chattering teeth.

"Plus, you might be interested in the new item I've added to my bucket list since we last spoke."

TOMMIE'S DREAM LOVER

Merina Canyon

I helped Liza load her boxes of books and clothes into her little run-down pickup, and when she said, "Come on, baby, go with me," I just tightened the bungee cords and kicked her tires. She was going off to college in Grand Junction and I was about to be left by the best girlfriend I ever had. Liza took hold of my shoulders and said, "Look at me, Tommie." And I tried, but my eyes bored holes in the tire tread. "I love you, you know," she said and kissed me hard. I pulled back. When Liza drove off down our gravel road, I stood out there, my hands in my pockets, kicking rocks. I felt like kicking myself.

Now I was standing in the red dust and grit alone, hearing a canyon wren laughing at me in the distance. I stayed outside for a couple of hours poking around in the desert and looking at junk in the shed. What the hell was I going to do? Without Liza, my life felt like an empty snakeskin. It used to hold life, but whatever thing had lived there had moved on and left me behind.

When I finally got up the courage to go inside, I just collapsed at the kitchen table with my head in my hands. I didn't blame Liza for wanting more out of life. She was smart and curious about everything—but me, I just wanted a girlfriend and a sense of home. I had lost both. My house was just an empty shell like me.

Right about then I heard a truck rumbling down the road. Like a kid I jumped up and ran to the door. In my mind it had to be Liza coming home to ask me one more time to go with her, and I might run out and say, *Move over. I'm driving.*

But it wasn't Liza's old pickup. It was Shelby's yellow Jeep—so new and shiny the red dust was afraid to settle on it.

I was standing in my doorway when Shelby swooped in and hollered, "Hey, Tommie girl."

"Hey, Shelby," I said. "What's up?"

"Did Liza leave already? I see you ain't gone with her."

"Yeah," I grumbled, kicking at dead cactus. "She's gone."

"You wish you'd gone with her?" Shelby never beat around the bush.

"I don't know, Shel. Don't ask me that."

"Listen, pal, when you want to talk, come out to my place. Don't sit around here by yourself." She tried to put a hand on my shoulder.

"I hear you," I said and turned all my attention to pulling cactus thorns out of the toe of my boot.

Shelby looked at me for a while, her hands on her hips, and then climbed back in the Jeep. "Least let me take you for a ride in my new baby here."

"Later," I said, but I didn't care about a new Jeep. I couldn't bear to picture what tomorrow would look like when I woke up and there's no Liza. Damn, I loved that girl with all my heart even if I didn't always show it. There could never be another woman like her.

Or could there?

That night I slouched on the back porch watching the sunlight creep down into the canyon until everything was that red-gray watercolor. A chill came with it—a chill I welcomed. I wrapped my arms around myself and cried. "God damn it, Liza, you knew I couldn't leave here. This is my home." Two or three bats skittered across the darkening sky hunting mosquitoes. Clouds filtered a little last purple-red light and then vanished. Stars started to pop—Venus, I think, and a few speckles. After two years of Liza living here with me, I was alone. Could I find a *new* dream lover?

And what would that dream lover look like? That's what I wanted to know. Would she be thin and small like Liza or would she be tall, dark and handsome like Xena: Warrior Princess? Would she like what I liked or would she be the total opposite of me?

I started to imagine this gorgeous woman from a South Pacific island with black hair rippling to her waist. She was coming toward me with an open coconut in her hands. A drink for me— the nectar of love and passion. Her name would have about twenty-five syllables in it, each one only two letters long—and she'd teach me how to say the name, but I'd never be able to say it right so I'd call just call her *Darling*.

I've always been good at fantasizing. Before Liza came along I would dream up a new lover every night, some with long hair, some with short, some crazy with passion, others reserved, waiting. But Liza, without knowing it, had put an end to my nighttime fantasies. That was the thing about Liza and me. When we were together, we were really together. No room for dream lovers when I had all I could handle and all I ever wanted right in front of me.

Liza and I met at Tucker's Gas Station, where I'd worked for almost five years. You might think that ain't much of a job, but

I was doing more than pumping gas—I practically ran the place, and I worked on cars. So Liza drove in one day in that old blue Toy pickup—you know how sometimes the word *Toyota* has been erased on the tailgate so that it just says *Toy*? That always made me laugh, and I was laughing as I started filling up her tank.

"What's so funny?" she asked out her window. She was wearing super-dark sunglasses, and her blond hair was all wind-blown.

"You have a cute little vehicle here, ma'am."

"Goddamn! Don't call me *ma'am*. Do I look like a ma'am to you?" She threw open her door and stepped out of the truck. She wore cut-offs so short that I could barely see them under her paisley peasant-girl shirt.

I apologized for being a jerk, and she said I could call her Liza.

"And so what do you get called around here, ma'am?" she said, playacting serious.

"Tommie. At your service."

"Tommie At Your Service? What was your mother thinking?"

Liza and I laughed over all sorts of dumb things. She was always a feisty woman—"ornery" is what some folks called her. To me she was just the nectar I needed. I noticed that I started standing up taller and I asked Shelby to cut my hair as cutely as possible. Shelby always cut my hair—she just had a talent for it—but after I met Liza, I thought Shelby was a little jealous. Shelby was a good friend to me so she took her time with my hair anyway. She even made me sit still for a highlight treatment. When she was all done she handed me a mirror and I smiled at myself.

"Damn," I said.

Shelby said, "Hot damn, sweetie pie. Come to mama!"

And when I picked up Liza that evening at her brother's

place where she was temporarily staying, she said, "Hey, cutie. Where's Tommie At Your Service?"

"She's busy tonight," I said. "Sent me to show you a good time."

"Sure she won't mind?"

"Hell, no."

You know how people say that lesbians go out on a first date and the next day they get out the pickups and move in together? That's just what happened with Liza and me. All of a sudden she didn't want to stay at her brother's anymore because him and his wife didn't approve of Liza dating another female, so she up and left. Nobody was going to tell her what she could and couldn't do. I love that about her.

We were dancing around my little kitchen, my hands up the back of her blouse unfastening her bra. In my fantasy she had already moved in. "I've got plenty of room, Liza. Stay here."

"You mean it, Tommie? You want me to live with you just like that?"

"Yeah, I want you to live with me. This can be *our* home."

"I think I love you," she said standing back and looking me in the eye, her bare breasts calling out to me. "I don't care if you're a woman or man. I just love you, you know?"

"Yeah, I know," I said. "But I *do* care you're a woman," and I pulled her into the bedroom. We almost broke the bed when we tumbled down.

Now Liza was gone. How did it happen? Was I too stubborn? I wanted to stay put whereas Liza needed to see the world. But first she wanted to go to school to study psychology. She thought the human mind was an endless marvel and she liked trying to figure people out, especially me.

The day after Liza left, I covered Melvin's shift at the gas station, and when Roger Dodger came in at five to let me go,

I didn't want to leave. I hung around talking to Roger Dodger until it got busy and then I took off. But I still didn't want to go home. And I wasn't hungry either. I could have had any food I wanted at the station, but I hadn't been hungry in days.

I started driving my Blazer aimlessly and ended up heading out to Shelby's place. My Blazer automatically went there like a farm animal heading for the barn.

I liked Shelby just fine—we'd been friends for a lot of years— but I really didn't want to talk about Liza leaving, even though I didn't want to go home and be alone. I just followed the Blazer's lead and got greeted by Shelby's little rescued golden retriever, Karma. The dog was crazy about me and I had to playact I was happy to see her. Shelby stood in the door waving me to come on in. She was working on something out back, so I followed her through her house and out the back door with Karma at my heels.

Shelby was working on some kind of fire pit. She had a pile of fist-sized stones she'd picked up in the desert and was about to mix some cement.

"I knew you'd come," Shelby said. "Didn't know if it would be today, but I was giving you forty-eight hours."

"Yeah, well, here I am," I said, flopping down in the lounge chair.

"Want something to eat?" Shelby offered without looking up. Karma licked my hand.

"Ain't hungry."

"When was the last time you ate?"

"Don't remember."

Shelby started talking about this rock sculpture she was making—some sort of goddess—Hera, I think she said, and she was all excited because some witchy women were coming out that very night to do a blessing ceremony. Shelby had two sides: One side was this no-nonsense cowgirl/landowner/I-can-take-anything side. The other was this goddess-worshipping/get-quiet-in-nature/ain't-life-a-mystery side. Good combination if you ask me. But right then I didn't feel like talking.

"Mind if I take a walk down Angel Canyon?"

"Be my guest," Shelby said. "But it's dark soon, so don't be gone long or I'll have to send Karma after you. In fact, take Karma with you."

"No, you keep her. I won't be gone long."

"Tommie, don't step on my rattlesnakes." That was Shelby's way of saying watch your step, and I said I would be careful.

Shelby knew I was being a fool setting off by myself into a red rock canyon full of slots and crumbling footholds and snakes and all that, and Shelby is always right.

I set out at a good clip like a mountain goat jumping from ledge to ledge, and I wandered down passageways. Always put me in mind of native folk surviving down there in the old days—and then the cowboys and settlers. Shelby was dang lucky to get that canyon with her property when she did. She always said it was a great place for a vision quest, what with all those pockets up high where you could sit and look out at the canyon maze.

Little did I know I was on a vision quest of my own. Even though I knew I was a fool, I just couldn't stop myself and turn back. I kept going deeper and felt brave and reckless at the same time. I pushed a big rock off a ledge and laughed—then felt scared. Were the spirits watching me and had I just disturbed their sanctuary? "Sorry," I said out loud.

I strayed out on a little red rock ledge and turned a corner. All of a sudden it was cool and lots darker. I'd gone too far and stayed too long. Where was I? That's when I tripped and fell down a slot.

I didn't think I hurt myself too bad, although I did taste

blood—and my wrist was throbbing like hell. The problem was I was down in a stone crevice too deep and smooth to climb out of. I kept thinking to jump and catch hold of something, but each time I did, I slid down and hurt my wrist worse.

"God damn it!" I yelled and felt all these critters and spirits listening to me. Were they all laughing?

I thought I heard a dog barking in the distance and I tried to call out *Karma!* But my voice went nowhere. It hit the rock wall I was practically kissing, and then it fell down around my feet, my mouth bleeding and my right arm feeling like it was twice its size.

"Liza," I whispered. "Liza, baby, don't leave me." I almost felt like I didn't say those words—like the words said themselves—like they were down deep inside me looking for an opportunity to climb out.

The next thing I knew it was pitch black. Somehow, though, I could see things before my eyes like I was dreaming. At first it was just objects appearing and disappearing—a rock, a fire, a hand, a feather, but then faces came up and looked so real that I lost my sense of being in the hole. I was somewhere else—a tropical island—and I could hear the ocean rolling in and out. There were drums too, and then voices, women's voices, and they were all whispering *Tom-mie, Tom-mie* like a heartbeat.

I could make out this misty figure looking like Shelby wearing a feathered headdress, and there were five other misty females looking like goddess worshippers dancing around a fire. Shelby was sitting like a Buddha but she was looking up into the sky and my name kept rising up—*Tom-mie, Tom-mie.*

But I was on a tropical island, right? I decided to walk toward the sound of the waves and see what might be there—*who* might be there. I felt like someone was waiting for me, a woman, and I had to go to her.

The closer I got, the clearer the image of this island woman became. She had her back to me—her black hair down to her waist—and I knew this was my dream lover. This was the woman the goddess wanted me to find and there she was waiting for me, the ocean waves reaching out to her bare feet. I wanted her to turn toward me, but she didn't turn when I said, "Darling?"

In fact, she started walking into the ocean and I called out, "No, don't go. Don't go!" But she ignored me and went anyway, and I realized I was so cold, trembling, shaking all over, and my dream lover went farther out to sea until the ocean waves went right over the top of her head.

I called out *No!* But she was gone.

I fell down on the beach and cried. How could she leave me? Oh goddess, help me.

Just then I made out a figure starting to emerge from the ocean. A blond head, a woman walking closer, a small-framed woman in a peasant blouse and no pants.

"Tommie," the woman said.

"Liza?" My Liza.

And she was bending over me with a worried look on her face. "I love you, you know," she said wiping tears off my face and pulling me up into her arms.

"Dream lover," I said.

"Uh-huh," she said. "I'm the one, dingbat."

And we both started laughing but I kept crying too and feeling cold, trembling, and then I saw those misty women around the circle again and Shelby with her feathers.

The next thing I knew I was opening my eyes deep down in the hole and I could see a little bit of morning light. I looked straight up and saw Karma's happy face and realized she had been barking a long time. I heard Shelby call my name and then she was there alongside Karma looking down at me.

"Damn, Tommie!" Shelby said like she'd seen a ghost. I knew she'd get me out. As I remember it, which ain't too clear, Shelby jumped down in that hole and braced me up against her. "Poor baby," I heard her say. Then her five witchy women friends hoisted us up and out with a rope, and one of them said, "Oh goddess," when she handled my wrist and I sobbed.

Six strong women carried me out of Angel Canyon with Karma hopping and dancing around us. That little dog knew she had saved my life.

Some of them wrestled me inside Shelby's yellow Jeep and we tore off to Grand Junction, the nearest hospital. I couldn't guzzle all the water I was handed, and it ran down the front of my bloodstained shirt.

Then things went quiet and I was out until I woke up in a hospital bed. I saw Shelby sitting by me with a phone in her hand like she was about to call someone. "Goddamn, Tommie, you scared the crap out of me. You're lucky Karma found you."

"Sorry," I said and tried to grin. "Tell Karma I said thanks." Then I started to drift off again. I could hear Shelby's voice but couldn't make out the words.

When I woke up for real I felt like I was being rocked in a cradle. Liza was wrapped around me like a cocoon and she was saying soft, sweet words and stroking my face.

"Darling?" I said.

And she jumped a little and said, "Tommie, you didn't need to go to all this trouble to get my attention!"

I tried to smile, but I knew that I *did* have to go to all this trouble to leave my old life and follow the sweet nectar offered to me in this new one. I knew now what I had to do. I would go along with Liza, and I'd let her show me the world.

UN-DRESS YOU UP IN MY LOVE

Allison Wonderland

"Sex-crazed straight girl preys on innocent lesbian. How's that for a headline?"

I'm clinging to her now, like one of those plush Garfields with the suction cups on its paws, the kind you stick on your car window. "I am *not* a heterosexual," I bristle, alternating between necking and nuzzling.

"You are according to that clock on the wall," Darla replies, pointing to the plastic pussycat with the tick-tock tail. "You're not officially a lesbian until your coming-out party."

Darla is referring to my impending debut. In less than an hour, we will be subverting (perverting?) a time-honored Southern tradition: the debutante ball. Darla had a conventional coming-out ceremony when she was eighteen. I did not, so she decided to make up for it. I thought the whole idea was kind of hokey and tried to dissuade her, but once an idea gets into Darla's head, it sticks there like a Post-it Note.

She's spent four months making the preparations. You should see our living room. It resembles the aftermath of a Skittles explosion. I appreciate all her hard work, but still...

"We could cancel it," I suggest, jiggling the zipper on her dress. "Once you've been to one ball, you've been to them all."

Darla's mouth takes the shape of an oval, reminiscent of an Easter egg. "Call off the ball?" she bawls, sounding at once melancholic and melodramatic. She jabs her fists onto her hips. "Heavens, no!"

I laugh, savoring the sound of her voice, all sugar and syrup and sass. She tried to ditch her accent once, tried to trade it for the timbre of the East Coast. (This happened shortly after we returned from a trip to the Big Apple. She says coincidence, I say hogwash.) But the North and the South just don't mix, and for all her efforts, she sounded like a cross between a vampire and a Valley Girl, which would have been cute if it hadn't been creepy. (I paid her—in sexual favors, of course—to say, "Like, oh, my gawd, I'm totally going to, like, suck your blood.")

I love her voice, *her* voice, in all its Georgian glory. And I love the way her lips move when she speaks, how they stretch and crinkle and smile—she can't seem to talk without smiling. And I love the way the apples of her cheeks puff up when she grins, especially when that grin is followed by a kiss. While we're on the subject of smooching, I love the way her kisses taste like pecan pie. And the way she holds me when she kisses me. And the way her fingers, long and limber, make me ache and quake and crumple.

Hard as it may be to believe, I didn't always feel this way about Darla. To be perfectly honest, when I first met her, I thought she was a trifle...repulsive.

Darla was the first to respond to the ad I'd placed in the local paper. I needed a new roommate, someone to share the cost of living with, someone with a mutual aversion to solitary confinement.

After chatting with Darla on the phone for a bit, I was anxious for her to arrive for an interview. And then she did, right on time, right on schedule, and I was anxious for Darla to leave.

There she stood, at the threshold of the apartment, clad in a denim skirt accented with lace and a turquoise blouse adorned with ruffles. Her wrists were shackled in baubles and pearls, her hair coiffed in hair spray and curls. An arsenal of adjectives sprang to mind as I inspected her: silly and frilly, prissy and sissy. She was the consummate material girl, all high heels and high style and high-maintenance.

She looked like a hybrid of Scarlett O'Hara and a French poodle.

Darla thrust her hand toward me, causing her bracelets to jangle like wind chimes. Trying to maintain some semblance of Southern hospitality, I shook her hand and invited her inside.

During the interview, Darla did all the talking and I did all the gawking. Right off the bat, I decided I had her number. I pegged Darla as the type of girl who would shriek at the sight of a bug, the type of girl who spent all of junior high and high school passing notes instead of taking them, the type of girl who was not my type.

"What do you do for a living?" I inquired, not sincerely interested, just curious.

"I'm not a socialite," she informed me, having detected the accusatory assumption in my tone. She crossed her ankles. "Y'know, Dixie, you really shouldn't judge a book by its cover," she scolded, a reprimand that, though clichéd, never fails to induce guilt. "I should know that better than anyone," she added, folding her hands in her lap. "I'm a librarian."

That revelation earned Darla due consideration, and our mid-morning interview continued into the afternoon and lingered into the evening.

"I think you decided to give me a second chance," Darla said, tipping the beverage bottle toward the glass, "because I was gracious enough to afford you the same courtesy." The soda slipped through the lips of the container and into the tumbler.

"I thought you accepted my apology," I pouted, taking the glass from her outstretched hand. "I never would have gone on this guilt trip in the first place if I'd known about the mandatory extended stay."

Darla smirked, flicking a balled-up napkin in my direction. "You want the last slice?"

I peered into the pizza box and shook my head. "Nah, it's yours. Have at it."

Darla pinched the crust between her fingers. Her nails were painted ladybug red, the polish applied in precise, perfect strokes. Something I have never been able to do.

"Hey," Darla said, nudging my elbow. My skin felt warm at the point of contact. "You haven't told me what you do."

"Oh, um, I'm a B.O. manager."

Darla regarded me with inquisitive eyes. Her gaze was bright green, like the inside of a kiwi. "You manage body odor for a living?"

"Box office," I clarified, the words squeezing past the frog in my throat. "I'm the box office manager for a theater."

"Movies or plays?"

"Plays."

"You'll have to take me to a show sometime." I nodded. "You shouldn't speak in shorthand," Darla counseled. "It's tacky." She stretched her legs out under the coffee table, flexed her toes, spotlighting the muscles in her calves. "So, what happened with your last roommate?"

I took a swig of soda to wash down the frog. "The dish ran away with the spoon," I answered.

"Does that mean that she absconded with your silverware or that she eloped with a silverware salesman?"

"More likely the latter. She was pretty much here and gone, only lasted about a month. Matter of fact, I didn't even catch her name."

Darla chuckled, her eyes dancing. "So, what's it going to be, girl? Have I got the part?"

I looked at Darla, beneath the bells and whistles this time. An arsenal of adjectives sprang to mind as I studied her: sweet and upbeat, kind and refined, witty and pretty.

Quite pretty.

"You can move in as soon as you want to."

Darla wrapped her arms around me, like thread twining a spool. "That's great, Dixie!"

I smiled when we separated. "Dixie and Darla," I mused. She chuckled. "We sound like a pair of country western crooners. Either that or a couple of roller-skating waitresses."

Darla laughed again, big and boisterous. The kind of laugh that made me feel like running in the rain.

I hate the rain.

I had an inkling I'd made a wise decision. Darla would bring a little luster, a little zing into my life. I started fantasizing about all the things she and I would share: gossip and girl talk, Dolly Parton and *Designing Women*. I could have kept my options open, could have kept looking—Darla was, after all, the first person who responded—but it just seemed like a waste of time.

Because whoever said that first is the worst had never met Darla.

Darla, I learned, was not exactly the most clothed person in the world. Even today, she has a habit of ambling around the apartment in her undergarments, which tend to push the line between hilarity and vulgarity. At any given moment, she will stride past me decked out in a sparkly, feathery garment that she swears is a nightshirt. Now I can admire her openly, but before it wasn't so easy.

I'd liked other girls—I'd dated other girls—but I liked this particular girl more than any other girl I'd ever liked before. I could spend eons talking to Darla about everything and nothing. I could tolerate all her little quirks, even the ones that were, by definition, intolerable, like her habit of dismissing the *Be Kind, Rewind* sticker on rental tapes.

What had started out as detestation changed to admiration. Admiration evolved into infatuation. And infatuation progressed to aspiration, meaning that I aspired to be something other than Darla's roommate and bosom buddy. The transformation happened gradually, as transformations often do, so it's difficult to pinpoint that crucial when-I-knew moment, though I sensed I was in deep trouble when Darla started calling me "honey pot" and I just ate it right up.

It didn't help that she had a fantastic figure: svelte and athletic, with gams that rivaled Betty Grable's and hips that looked like they could keep a Hula-Hoop rotating for hours. And it certainly didn't help that we shared a room. All it did was aid and abet my wandering eyes.

My gaze became particularly incorrigible at night, with Darla in the adjacent twin bed, dozing in one of her "nightshirts." She faced me when she slept, which meant I had to look at her when I touched myself, because no way in the world was I going to close my eyes or turn my back and risk getting caught wet-handed.

I wondered how it would feel to have and to hold her. I wondered what it'd be like to experience the bliss of our first kiss. I wondered if...

I wondered if I'd ever muster up the courage to tell her how I felt.

A few months later, I almost mustered up the courage. There we were, sitting in the audience of the theater, waiting for the curtain to rise on a revival of *A Streetcar Named Desire*. Mentally, I prepared to make my first move. I closed my eyes and imagined there was a tiny cheerleader perched on my shoulder, rustling her pom-poms and bellowing words of encouragement: *You can do it, you can do it, you can, you can.* I'm well aware that the movie theater is the standard setting for first moves, but the lights were already dimmed and the seats were really comfortable, so I didn't think I would have too much trouble adapting.

Until it occurred to me that I had far fewer options in a theater than I had at the movies. I couldn't reach into the bucket of popcorn at the same time Darla did and accidentally-on-purpose touch her hand. I couldn't drape my arm over the back of her chair and then ever so subtly move my hand from her seat to her shoulder to her sweater. Well, I could have, I suppose, but I would not have dared.

I could have tried to hold her hand. That I could have done. It was right there, right next to me on the armrest. Her fingers were curved slightly, like the stems of her sunglasses. Every time those fingers moved, it felt like they were taunting me to touch them, to take them, to press them into my palm.

I spent the entire performance slumped in my seat, cursing my clammy hands and cold feet. I was a lily-livered loser, completely unworthy of the fetching, self-confident belle I bunked with.

After the show, I couldn't exit the theater fast enough. I wanted nothing more than to get home, get into bed and begin the excruciating process of getting over Darla.

"Did you enjoy the play, Dix?" Darla asked, struggling to keep pace.

I was testy and ticked off and I took it out on her. "Don't call me that," I muttered.

Darla tittered. "Oh, now you're too good for nicknames, is that it? C'mon, Dix, don't be so cocky."

I didn't answer, just walked faster, the soles of my boots slapping the pavement.

"Hey." She latched onto my arm, yanking me to a sudden stop. Reluctantly, I raised my head to look at her. Darla's face was all lines—her lips, the space between her eyes. I couldn't read her. "Do you like me? And don't say 'Of course I like you,' like you've got no idea what I'm talking about." She paused. I panicked. "Back there," she said, when I said nothing, "in the theater, you wanted to hold my hand, didn't you?"

"I...um..."

"Did you or didn't you?"

"I...did."

"If you did, then why didn't you?"

"I...just didn't."

"Dixie, you know I'm a lesbian, right?"

I felt grateful that she hadn't released her grip on my arm. Otherwise, I would have taken a nasty spill onto the sidewalk.

Did I, Dixie, know that she, Darla, was a lesbian? I had wondered about it and wished for it and even allowed myself to suspect that she might possibly be a teensy bit bi. But know? No, I didn't know. Armed with this new and very valuable information, I hadn't the slightest idea how to respond. I couldn't manage a stammer or a smile or a shake of the head. All I could manage to do was utter a feeble "Okay."

Darla just about had a hissy fit. "What in the world is the matter with you?" She jabbed me in the shoulder with the pointy, painted tip of her fingernail. "How can you stand there and say a thing like that? I'm hurt, Dixie, I'm truly hurt. Not to mention I'm terribly disappointed in you. I was looking forward to a good old-fashioned Southern swooning, y'know? Whip out your handkerchief and wave it around and cry, 'Mercy me!' or 'I declare!' and then, once you've gotten all that out of your system, pucker up and plant one on me."

All I could manage to do was utter a feeble "Okay."

But that time, Darla didn't give a damn.

"For she's a jolly good lesbo, for she's a jolly good lesbo, for she's a jolly good lesbo...which nobody can deny..."

My coming-out party, the social event of the season, as Darla put it, has been in progress for two hours and counting. I've spent the bulk of that time smiling and mingling and pretending that I'm not thinking about screwing my sweetheart senseless as soon as this soiree is over.

Attempts to conserve my energy and preserve my sanity have all but failed, what with Darla's constant demands to dance and my parents' barrage of self-aggrandizing anecdotes. (To their credit, my folks have come a long way, having finally grown out of the it's-just-a-phase phase. I just think it's high time they stopped patting themselves on the back about it.)

Somehow, someway, my debut draws to a close, and one by one the guests trickle out of the apartment. No sooner has the door closed than Darla is dragging me into the kitchen, tugging my hand as if I'm a pull toy. "That was some shindig, huh?" she remarks as she hands me a stack of plates and directs me to the sink.

We have to do this now? Wouldn't it be more prudent to get down and dirty and *then* get spic and span? I decide not to air my grievances—why waste precious time?—and we begin to scrub in silence, all the while exchanging glances and giggles and intangible love notes.

Fifteen minutes later, Darla slaps the dishrag down onto the counter. "That's it. I'm throwing in the towel." She pushes her bangs out of her eyes. I exhale, exhausted, and peel off my rubber gloves. "I don't know what you're sighing about, honey pot," Darla scolds. "Wiping is far more taxing than washing."

"It's my party and I'll sigh if I want to." I suppress a giggle. I slump against the sink. "So, am I officially a lesbian now?"

Darla claps her hands. "Gimme an *L*, gimme an *E*, gimme an *S*, *BIAN*! What does that spell? Lesbian!"

I can't help but get a little misty. "You should start your own pep squad," I suggest, adjusting the cap on the bottle of dish-washing soap. "You can call it Cheers for Queers."

Darla laughs and slings her arm around my waist. "You're just lucky we have the good sense to keep the front door locked at all times. What would have happened if the guests had walked in and found us rolling around on the floor like a couple of lady wrestlers?"

"We didn't get that far," I remind her. "But if we had, I reckon they would've wanted to get in on the action."

Darla lassos me in. I nearly bang into her bosom. We are so close I can no longer distinguish my heartbeat from hers. Darla grins, all impish eyes and impatient hands. "Pucker up and plant one on me," she says, uttering the command that has become our signature smooch starter.

I don't know whose bed we're lying on, or how long we've been in bed, or how we even got into the bedroom in the first place. I never know. All I know is that I want more of Darla's kisses, the sensation of her lips, gentle yet manic. I love the way her kisses make my insides turn soft and mushy, like banana pudding.

The advent of our ardor is accompanied by the roving of

hands, the removal of clothing. Her fingers drift along my naked body, from the knolls of my breasts to the knot of my navel.

I emulate her movements, guiding my palm along the planes of her midriff. Her skin has a silky, supple feel to it, like the texture of hair ribbons.

Darla's fingers make a swift shift to my sex. Lust whips through me as her fingers plunge inside. My body aches and quakes and crumples.

"Care to lend a hand, Dix?" she murmurs.

"The pleasure is all mine."

"That's how come I asked." Darla seizes my wrist and squeezes my hand between her thighs. She is warm and moist, with the sticky splendor of peach cobbler.

I smile against her kiss. I'm starting to get that fuzzy, dizzy, on-the-brink-of-an-orgasm feeling when Darla's fingers are gone, and then, so are mine.

She moves so that her body is blanketing me, our limbs spliced like a licorice vine. I soak in her scent: part apple cider, part wild honeysuckle.

We dance together, her leading, me following. But as we progress, our movements begin to coincide, our souls begin to coexist.

Friction begets frenzy.

Gasps evolve into laconic whispers.

Our release comes abruptly, drenching us with heat and honey.

"I love you."

I don't know which of us said it.

But I know both of us meant it.

THE LAST RAYS OF THE SUMMER SUN

Andrea Dale

It was Angel's turn to do the supper dishes.

Up until last month, our twins, Kelly and Jacob, had shared dish duty. But with both of them off to college now, we were back to Angel and me trading off.

Strange, the little things that change when your kids leave home.

The dishes had actually piled up for a few days before we remembered to negotiate the chore, along with a few others left in the twins' wake. We'd also had to get used to the silence: no more of Kelly and Jacob's voices, music, footfalls down the stairs, or impassioned cell phone conversations.

Then again, there had been a few positive changes, too.

We'd replaced the silence with our favorite '80s tunes, breaking into spontaneous dance or song with no child to roll his or her eyes.

We'd also slowly defaulted back to our pre-kid clothing choices, or near lack thereof. In the annual Southern California autumn heat wave, I was wearing a gray cotton sports bra and a pair of loose running shorts, and admiring the way the evening sun shone through Angel's thin sundress.

She wasn't wearing anything underneath it.

It was a cliché, but I'd always thought my Angel looked like her namesake, her red-gold hair now burnished by the setting sun, her curvy hips and thighs outlined beneath her sheer skirt.

As quickly as that thought entered my mind, another one chased it away. Fallen angel, more like it. She'd always been a delicious mix of curious and inventive in bed (and out of it), and a slow warmth pooled in my groin as the clock in the entryway chimed 7 P.M. and I remembered something I'd almost forgotten.

But before I could say anything, Angel wiped her hands on a cobalt and white checked dishtowel, turned to me, and said, "Time for *Jeopardy!*"

And from the wicked glint in her brown eyes, I knew we were having the same thought.

Once the twins were old enough to have a bedtime past 7 P.M., Angel and I stopped playing our *Jeopardy* sex game. When they were old enough to enjoy the game show, we invented a chores version of the game, but by high school and various after-school activities on top of homework, they'd moved on, and Angel and I had never really picked it up again, spending our evenings with email and whatnot before kicking back with a police drama or sitcom.

You do the math. It had been a long time.

My body, though, hadn't forgotten. My bra felt suddenly tight as my breasts swelled, my nipples peaking. Eager, hopeful...time to play?

I grabbed the remote and found the channel as Angel came in from the kitchen. "Strip, baby," she said.

"Race you," I countered. "Before the credits are over."

The theme song sent a second frisson of heat zinging at my pussy. The race wasn't really fair. All Angel had to do was pop the bow at the back of her neck and tug her sundress off, so she was naked when I'd just barely gotten my damn bra unhooked.

"Penalty to Team Marisol!" She laughed and dropped onto the sofa next to me.

I didn't even think about protesting that we hadn't discussed ground rules. After all, I'd suggested the strip race...knowing I'd lose.

The rules had always been a bit fluid anyway. Whoever answered the question first, before both the other person and the TV contestant, won a point. If one of us answered the question first but incorrectly, though, that person received a penalty.

There were other rules, for Daily Doubles and Final Jeopardy and whatnot, but that was the gist of it.

The rewards and penalties, of course, depended on our whims. When we'd started, it actually hadn't been sexual. More like who had to do dishes, or one of us giving the other a foot rub. That hadn't lasted long, though. We were young, in love, and very, very frisky.

Now she immediately demanded one of those foot rubs as my penalty. I dug my thumbs gently into the balls of her feet as she wiggled her toes with delight. Alex Trebek introduced the contestants, then the categories, explaining the rules we knew by heart.

When you've been with someone a long time, you kind of stop looking at them. Or maybe it's that you stop seeing them. If you blindfolded me, I could describe every curve of Angel's body, every line, every mole; the spots that were ticklish, the areas that were always warm or always cool; the way she smelled, the breathy hitch in her voice when she was aroused.

But when was the last time I'd actually *looked*?

Tonight felt ('80s cliché warning) like the first time.

I was utterly charmed and fascinated by the tiny furrow between her brows as she considered a question. I felt besotted and breathless once again with the curve of her collarbone, the dusky hardness of her nipples, the rounded pooch of her belly, the softness of her inner arm as I stroked it with my fingertips. I felt dizzy with desire in a way I'd forgotten, and hadn't realized I'd forgotten until now.

Desire is fucking distracting, too, so I was missing questions left and right.

"What's up with you tonight?" Angel asked at the first commercial break.

"Just…distracted," I said. I started to explain, then stopped. How to put it into words? Instead, I abandoned her foot and slowly slid one hand up her smooth calf.

She caught her breath, her eyes fluttering shut for a moment. She shifted on the sofa, and I caught a whiff of her special scent, spicy and *her*. In echoing response, my own pussy flooded with moisture. I rose to my knees and leaned over her for a kiss, cupping her breast in my hand and feeling her nipple stiffen into my palm.

I was intent on her pleasure, which certainly brought *me* pleasure, but perhaps not quite as intensely. The way I figured it, I probably owed her due to my muffing so many questions. I swear I didn't have an ulterior motive.

I swear it didn't occur to me until the next round started, and Angel's brain was so lust-fogged that *she* screwed up several questions in a row, all in American History, a category she knew well.

Maybe if I kept distracting her…

Of course, Angel was sharp as a tack—one of the things I adore about her—and soon she was on to my trick. Things promptly dissolved into each of us trying to distract the other through carnal shenanigans. While still trying to answer questions.

My mouth on her breast, I mumbled, "What is MARTA?"

Her teeth gently tugging at my earlobe, she murmured, "Who is Styx?"

My thigh between hers, bearing down, I crooned, "What is *The Scarlet Pimpernel*?"

Her fingernails grazing my back, she gasped, "What is the Waldorf-Astoria?"

We were neck-and-neck (as near as I could keep count, which wasn't very much) when we rolled into Final Jeopardy. The category was Authors. This was my forte. I was golden. I moaned that I'd bet it all. That was my mistake.

Before the commercial break was over, Angel somehow had me pinned down, her three fingers crooked inside me, beckoning me closer and closer to orgasm.

Alex Trebek said, "What literary group met at the Eagle and Child pub, familiarly known as the Bird and Baby?"

My stomach muscles tensed and my thighs trembled. I knew this...

Angel stroked deep inside me. I wasn't just having trouble thinking—I was losing language completely.

The music dum-de-dummed closer to the finish.

My body thrummed closer to orgasm.

"Oh...fuck...yes...The Inklings!"

The red wash of orgasm crashed over me, my screams drowning out the music and even the answer as my body pulsed and shuddered and succumbed.

There really are no winners or losers in this game. Dimly I heard Angel chuckling. "You forgot to say 'Who were'..." She tsk'd. "When you've recovered, I believe it's my turn."

My liquid limbs would resolidify in a few moments, and yes, then it would be her turn. I would make my sweet Angel sing to the heavens as many times as I possibly could.

We'd been together a long time, Angel and me. Long enough to have twins in college—Angel had carried them. Long enough to get married when we were finally allowed to, having known that whole time that it was forever for us. It's easy to slip into routines, to stop paying attention, to get dragged down by life and work and family, once the first heated rush of passion has slowed to a glowing pile of embers.

As *Jeopardy* ended and *Wheel of Fortune*'s audience chant began, the flames rose up again to meet the last rays of the summer sun. We wouldn't let them die down again so easily.

STAYING POWER

Radclyffe

She caught me watching her again this morning. I was out riding the Toro, trimming the bridle paths around the pastures. She was exercising a jumper she was planning to take to Devon in a couple of weeks, working him in the ring on combinations. She wasn't dressed in show clothes, just the jeans and T-shirt and dusty boots she wore around the farm every day, but she looked every bit as elegant astride the black beauty as she did in jodhpurs and jacket. Her shoulder-length blond hair was pulled back and held at the base of her neck with a simple black tie, and she'd looped a red bandana around her neck. It was hot, way too hot even for August—the air still and heavy, and by ten in the morning my T-shirt was already soaked through between my shoulder blades and my jeans were damp along the inside of my thighs. Watching her didn't make me any cooler. Sunlight glistened on the small beads of sweat on her bare forearms and I envisioned catching them on my tongue. I imagined a faint trickle of moisture trailing down her throat and pooling in a crystal droplet at the hollow between her collarbones where I'd place my first kiss.

I'd lucked out when my kid brother got a surprise athletic scholarship for the summer and went off to soccer camp and I got his farm job. Suddenly, I was the farm boi, and I couldn't be happier. I spent the day working outside and never had to worry about exercising or what I ate, and I got to watch her all day long. I tried to be subtle about it, but I guess I probably failed, because every now and then I'd notice this glint in her eye that made me think she knew exactly what I was thinking. And then I'd blush again. Because what I was thinking was definitely X-rated. It's not like I was some kind of pathetic social misfit who couldn't get a date—I dated, sort of, casually, now and then. But I wasn't really interested in anyone…else. I was interested in her. Like she would ever notice me—I'd just finished college and my immediate plans were go to work with my dad and my older brother in the construction business after taking the summer off. That was until I got to be farm boi. Now my immediate plans were a lot different.

I slowed the big mower while she took the last few jumps, her body arched over Thunder's withers, her power and his perfectly attuned. I must've slowed too much without realizing it and the Toro stalled, grinding to a halt with an obnoxious backfire. She glanced my way as Thunder cleared the posts with plenty to spare and my face got redder than the heat could account for. Busted.

That seemed to happen a lot—her catching me standing, probably open-mouthed, just looking. And okay, fantasizing. I'd wondered what she wondered about it. It's not like she wasn't used to being cruised—everyone did it—the mailman, the guy who picked up the trash, the farrier, everybody—she was gorgeous. I don't think she noticed them looking, or if she did, she never let on. She was pleasant to everyone, businesslike, friendly, but a little remote. She always had something on the agenda—something that needed to be done and, as the summer wore on, something she wanted me to do, more often than not. These past few weeks I'd been getting to work earlier and staying later, sometimes until after dusk. Lately, she'd been asking me to join her out on the rough stone patio behind the farmhouse for dinner, seeing as how she always grilled plenty. Those nights I'd wash up in the tack room and grab a clean T-shirt from my truck and try my best to be smart and engaging and not stare, for crying out loud.

I tried not to read too much into those dinners. I couldn't imagine why she'd be interested—I was okay-looking—I looked just like my brothers, everyone said—dark hair, dark eyes, big and sturdy—healthy farm stock. I rowed in college so my shoulders were pretty good and I wasn't carrying any extra weight, or at least I'd burned off what I'd picked up at school pretty fast hauling and cutting and forking all day long. But she was sophisticated, worldly, used to being in charge—hell, she ran the whole damn place by herself—not to mention gorgeous. I'd never seen her with anyone, but I couldn't imagine she didn't have somebody. How could she not?

I got the Toro going again just as she was finishing up in the ring, and I took the mower back and parked it in the lean-to attached to the big barn while she took Thunder inside to wipe him down and feed him. I was just walking by the open door when I heard her call my name.

"Yeah?" I called back.

She appeared in the doorway, her blue eyes dancing, her mouth so kissable I had to work at not staring. Again.

"Can you give me a hand for a minute back here? There's a couple of things in the loft I want to get down and Jim never got around to repairing the ladder last week. I just need you to steady it for a minute."

"Sure," I said, following her back inside the cool, dim barn. The scent of sweet clover and hay filled the air. I thought about summer wheat fields and lazy afternoons in the shade. I thought about her ass, tight and taunting, as she strode ahead of me in her worn jeans and dusty boots. The wooden ladder to the hayloft was maybe fifteen feet tall, just a simple series of two-by-fours nailed to vertical uprights. A couple steps were loose and the uprights had been needing shoring up where they joined the platform overhead. She stepped up onto the second rung and looked down at me over her shoulder. "If this thing starts coming down, you get out of the way. I'll jump clear."

"If this thing starts coming down, I'll catch you."

She grinned. "Then you better be as strong as you look."

My mouth went dry. I grasped the ladder on either side of her thighs, and that brought my chest almost up against her backside. She didn't start climbing, just studied me with a dark serious look, a few loose blond strands teasing down along her neck where I wanted my lips to be.

"I am," I said, my head tilted back to see her better. Her gaze drifted down along my throat, and my voice broke. "Plenty strong enough. I've got great stamina, so I've been told."

"I believe it," she said, her mouth turning up at one corner.

My clit started to pulse. I'd been waiting for this opportunity all summer—but as much as I'd fantasized about it, as many times as I'd come thinking about it, I never thought I'd get the chance to touch her. I leaned closer until my chest nestled against her legs. She watched me, now, her lids lowered, her lips parted as if waiting for a kiss. I wasn't being subtle—I wanted her to know I wanted her.

Slowly, she turned on the ladder, her thigh brushing across my nipples as she pivoted around until her ass was against the rungs and the zipper of her jeans was opposite my face. She couldn't possibly miss the hard round impression of my nipples through my thin tank. I couldn't swallow around the lump of want in my throat. I shifted my grip from the worn wooden ladder to the firm curve of her hips. Her fingers came into my hair.

"This is a bad idea," she said, her voice husky.

I stroked up and down the outside of her legs, and her tight rider's muscles quivered. I heard a tiny catch in her breath and everything inside me went liquid and hot. "Why?"

She sifted strands of my hair through her fingers, ruffling the short waves, restless little tugs that made my clit jump as if she was stroking between my legs.

"I'm too old for you," she said matter-of-factly, no apology in her voice.

I laughed and surprise flickered across her face. "*That's* why it's a bad idea? You're older?"

"About twenty years older."

"Well, lucky me then, since I'll be the one you're touching now, and considering all those years of practice, you'll be damn good at it."

Her smile widened. "Is that right?"

I worked free the snap on her fly and her hips give a little surge. "That's right. A little later."

"I told myself I wasn't going to do this," she said, one hand on my shoulder, the other on my neck. Her fingers were hot.

"Why?" I asked again, pulling each button free until I parted her jeans.

"Because I've wanted you since the day you walked up the drive," she murmured, "and I'm going to have a hard time forgetting you as it is. If you finish what you've started, I'm not sure I can."

I kissed the smooth, tanned skin of her belly. "Oh, I'm gonna finish. Not today, though." She gave a tiny sound of protest that came out a lot like a growl and I grinned, happy to know I wasn't the only one going a little bit insane with need. "It's gonna take me a long time to finish everything I want to do to you."

"Then you'd better get started. I don't think I can wait the rest of the summer."

"Done," I whispered and eased her jeans down enough so I could kiss my way down the center of her belly to the V between her legs. She was sweet and hot like fresh-cut grass, as rich as newly turned earth in the noontime sun. I kissed her and she whispered yes, and I took her in my mouth. She was already full and hard and her thighs trembled against my breasts as I took her deeper. Her fingers dug into my shoulders, and I held her hips tighter, keeping her close against my mouth. I'd waited too long to go slowly, but I tried. I wanted her to feel my wonder, my joy, but she gripped my head and pulled me hard against her and said, "I'm going to come for you very soon. It feels too good."

And I couldn't ask her to wait. There'd be time enough to go slow the next time. She cried out and her hips lurched and I strengthened my hold to keep her steady on the rickety old ladder. When she quieted, I rested my cheek against her belly and listened to the soft sound of her breathing and the shuffle of the horses in their stalls and the distant cry of a bird.

"How could I forget," she whispered, her fingers trembling against my cheek.

I licked salt from her skin and gazed up at her. "If you think you might, let me know so I can do it again."

She smiled, sadness in her eyes. "If there's never another time, I just want you to—"

"There will be." I knew all the reasons she could give me why we were a bad idea, but one thing everybody always said about me was I had tremendous staying power. And I planned on staying. For as long as it took for her to believe me.

ABOUT THE AUTHORS

METTE BACH (www.mettebach.com) contributed to *Visible: A Femmethology, First Person Queer, Second Person Queer* and *Fist of the Spider Woman*. She used to think lesbian romance was an oxymoron but she's wiser now.

This is the first Cleis anthology featuring a story by **JOEY BASS** and she hopes it won't be the last. She was raised on a tiny farm in suburban Southern California with her five siblings. Joey is joyfully civilized and leading a quiet life in the UK with her partner.

CHEYENNE BLUE's (www.cheyenneblue.com) erotica has appeared in many anthologies, including *Best Women's Erotica, Mammoth Best New Erotica, Best Lesbian Erotica* and *Best Lesbian Romance*. She currently lives in Queensland, Australia, but plans on living in Spain once she stops mangling the language.

MERINA CANYON lives it up in the red rock wonderland of Moab, Utah. She loves storytelling, desert meditations and long journeys into nature. Her stories have appeared in *Best Lesbian Romance 2011*, *Best Lesbian Love Stories 2009* and *2010*, *Sinister Wisdom 76* and *83*, *Fraglit.com* and *Pilgrimage Press vol. 36*.

Called a "legendary erotica heavy-hitter" (by the über-legendary Violet Blue), **ANDREA DALE** (www. cyvarwydd.com) writes sizzling erotica with a generous dash of romance. Her work has appeared in *Lesbian Cowboys: Erotic Adventures* and Romantic Times 4.5-star *Fairy Tale Lust*, as well as anthologies from Harlequin Spice, Avon Red and Cleis Press. .

CHARLOTTE DARE's erotic fiction has appeared in *Best Lesbian Romance 2010*, *Best Lesbian Erotica*, *Lesbian Cowboys*, *Girl Crazy*, *Ultimate Lesbian Erotica*, *Wetter: More True Lesbian Sex Stories*, *Where the Girls Are* and in various online publications. As always, she thanks her red-hot lover Ana for her endless inspiration.

DELILAH DEVLIN (www.delilahdevlin.com) is an award-winning author of erotic romance with a rapidly expanding reputation for writing edgy stories with complex characters. She has published over a hundred stories from Avon, Berkeley, Kensington, Cleis Press and others.

KATE DOMINIC is a former technical writer who now writes about much more interesting ways to put parts together. She is the author of over 300 short stories and is considerably more fond of wearing silk camisoles and thermals than she is of ice fishing.

ARIEL GRAHAM lives with her husband in northern Nevada. A full-time writer, her work has appeared in multiple anthologies including *Please, Sir* and *Please, Ma'am*, as well as online at Torquere, Oysters & Chocolate and Pink Flamingo.

SACCHI GREEN's (www.sacchi-green.blogspot.com) stories have appeared in a hip-high stack of publications with erotically inspirational covers, and she's also edited or co-edited eight erotica anthologies, including *Girl Crazy*, *Lesbian Cowboys* (winner of the 2010 Lambda Literary Award for lesbian erotica,) *Lesbian Lust*, *Lesbian Cops* and *Girl Fever*, all from Cleis Press.

C.J. HARTE is an incurable romantic who doesn't want to be cured. Her lesbian romances *Dreams of Bali* and *Magic of the Heart* are available from Bold Strokes Books.

L.T. MARIE (www.ltmarie.com) is a career athlete and author. Her first book *Three Days* is available from Bold Strokes Books.

ANNA MEADOWS is a part-time executive assistant, part-time housewife. She writes from her heritage in the Mexican-American Southwest and her passion for stories about women in love. Her work appears in thirteen anthologies. She lives with her Sapphic husband in California.

CATHERINE PAULSSEN (www.catherinepaulssen.com) loves winter, licorice, old Hollywood movies, Motown music, and cooking for friends and family. Her stories have been published by Cleis Press, Silver Publishing and Constable & Robinson.

ALLISON WONDERLAND (aisforallison.blogspot.com) is one L of a girl. Her lesbian literature appears in *Milk and Honey*,

Bound by Lust, *Girl Fever* and *Locker Room*. In addition to Sapphic storytelling, Allison's indulgences include cotton candy, kitten heels and Old Hollywood glamour.

Originally from Atlanta, Georgia, **DIANE WOODROW** now lives in upstate New York with her partner of twenty years and their two kids. She is a freelance technical writer by trade.

ABOUT THE EDITOR

RADCLYFFE has written forty romance, romantic intrigue, and, as L.L. Raand, paranormal romance novels; authored dozens of short stories; and edited multiple anthologies. She is an eight-time Lambda Literary Award finalist in romance, mystery and erotica—winning in romance (*Distant Shores, Silent Thunder*) and erotica (*Erotic Interludes 2: Stolen Moments* edited with Stacia Seaman and *In Deep Waters 2: Cruising the Strip* written with Karin Kallmaker). *Best Lesbian Romance 2010* from Cleis Press was a Lambda finalist. She is an inductee of the Saints and Sinners Literary Hall of Fame, an RWA/FF&P Prism award winner, a Benjamin Franklin and ForeWord Review Book of the Year award finalist, and as L.L. Raand, the RWA Passionate Plume award finalist. She is also the president of Bold Strokes Books, one of the world's largest independent LGBT publishing companies.